PUFF...

Somed...

Elaine Forrestal was born in Perth, Western Australia, but has lived in many different places and travelled throughout the world. Apart from Australia, she has spent most time in France, Northern Ireland, England and Canada. Her two daughters are now grown up. Elaine's husband is also a writer, so he udnerstands the peculiar demands of the occupation.

Being both a writer and teacher, Elaine is able to keep close contact with a wide range of children, and many of her story ideas spring from school experiences. She has had magazine articles and short stories published and has written for children's television. Her novel *Watching the Lake* was shortlisted for the Western Australian Premier's Book Awards.

Someone
Like Me

Elaine Forrestal

PUFFIN BOOKS

PUFFIN BOOKS

Published by the Penguin Group
Penguin Books Ltd, 27 Wrights Lane, London W8 5TZ, England
Penguin Books USA Inc., 375 Hudson Street, New York, New York 10014, USA
Penguin Books Australia Ltd, Ringwood, Victoria, Australia
Penguin Books Canada Ltd, 10 Alcorn Avenue, Toronto, Ontario, Canada M4V 3B2
Penguin Books (NZ) Ltd, 182–190 Wairau Road, Auckland 10, New Zealand

Penguin Books Ltd, Registered Offices: Harmondsworth, Middlesex, England

First published in Australia by Penguin Books Australia Ltd 1996
Published in Great Britain in Puffin Books 1997
1 3 5 7 9 10 8 6 4 2

Filmset in Baskerville

Made and printed in England by Clays Ltd, St Ives plc

British Library Cataloguing in Publication Data
A CIP catalogue record for this book is available from the British Library

ISBN 0-140-38644-0

For Russ and Bon,
my father and mother,
who passed on to me their love of books and music

My thanks to the real Thomas Alexander St John Kennedy for permission to use his name, and to the real Tas, who will recognize himself in the story although he is not named here. Also to Phil Hatton, music specialist extraordinaire, for his advice and involvement in the whole process, and to Julie Watts, Erica Irving and Karen McPhie for their endless patience and unshakeable belief in this book. To Peter Forrestal, thanks for *not* reading the manuscript *or* putting in those extra commas.

Chapter 1

'Come here! Now!' It's the new teacher. She's caught me eating my lunch round the corner in the sun – out of bounds. 'What's your name?' That means she's going to write it in the punishment book.

'Thomas Alexander St John Kennedy.' I say it really fast. Maybe she'll write it down wrong and they won't know it's me.

'Big name for a small boy,' she says.

'I'm not *that* small.' That makes it worse. Sometimes I should just keep my mouth shut.

'Right. Stay in after school. Ten minutes for being out of bounds and another ten for insolence.'

'I can't stay in after school, Miss. I go home on the bus.'

'Well you can start your detention *now*. Go

and sit on the bench outside the office for the rest of lunch-time.'

Rats. Another lunch-time wasted.

As I round the corner I can already hear him. 'Will you look who's here. Tas Kennedy. What a surprise.'

It's Dreadlock. He's already on the bench. Dreadlock is not his real name. I just call him that because he's got these tight curls that go into ringlets when his hair gets a bit long. He hates it. But his mother never wants them cut off. I go to clobber him, but he sticks his arm up.

'Shut up, Dreadlock. Anyway, you can't talk. You were here first. What did you get caught for? Being out of your coffin in broad daylight?'

'Running on the paving.' We wouldn't normally talk to each other, but there's nothing else to do, stuck on this bench. 'Soppy Miss what's-her-name caught me.'

'Watson.'

'What?'

'Miss Watson, thick-o. That's her name.'

'Oh, yeah.'

The minutes drag by. Other kids are laughing, playing games, having fun.

'She got me, too,' I say eventually. 'Wrote my name in the book.'

'And mine,' he says glumly. 'That's twice this week and it's only Wednesday.' If you get your name in the book more than three times in a week, they call your parents.

'I reckon I can fix her, though.' An idea has started wriggling around in my head.

'Yeah, yeah,' he says. 'You couldn't fix a cold drink in an igloo. Anyway, we're not even in her class, so how you gonna get at her, eh?'

'Bet I can!'

'Bet you can't, pipsqueak!' He slides up close and gives me a shove. I shove him back, but he's a lot heavier than me. He hooks his leg under mine and we roll off the bench together. We pummel each other on the paving. The bricks are hard and hot from the sun.

Then the siren goes. I dash for the loo. I'll be in trouble with Mr Mac for being late to class. But I'd be in even more trouble if he found a puddle of pee on his classroom carpet.

When I get to our room everyone is sitting at their desks. I try to walk in quietly, but Mr Mac says, 'Ah, the late Mr Kennedy.' He's not that bad, Old Mac, but his jokes are a bit off sometimes.

'Jest carl me JFK,' I say in my best American accent.

'Ssh,' Enya says. She can't handle the aggro. Not used to it, like I am. I don't know how she does it. Stay out of trouble, I mean. But she does, and she still manages to be a really neat kid with it.

Enya hasn't lived here for ever, like me. When she first came, Kristy latched on to her. Kristy is always looking for a new friend. She wears out her old ones pretty quickly. Smothers them with attention. Gives them presents. Invites them to her house. Swarms all over them. Then the novelty wears off and she goes on to someone else. They've usually had enough of her by then anyway, so it's okay.

But Enya's different.

On her first day here, Kristy moved in. The direct approach.

'Come and eat your lunch over here, with us.'

Most new kids are so grateful for the offer they break the land speed record getting over there.

'No thanks,' says Enya. 'I want to finish m' book so I can change it today.'

How about that? Miss Josephine Cool Incorporated. She sits on her own, reading her book. But now it's not only Kristy who's interested. Other kids gather round.

'What book is it?'

'Must be good.'

'Give us a look.' They start jostling her.

If they did that to me, I'd push their teeth down to their tonsils. But not Enya.

'It's just getting interesting,' she says. 'It's about these kids in a tunnel that keeps tilting and spinning them out into other time zones.'

'Sounds weird.'

'Can I read it after you?'

'It's not mine. I have to give it back.'

'Whose is it then?'

But she's not listening any more. That's how it is with Enya. She does her own thing.

I'm the last kid to get on the bus at home time. Dreadlock messed me around again. Pinched my calculator. By the time I give him a Chinese burn and force him to give it back, and Mr Mac tells us off for fighting, Mr Greenwood, our bus driver, has the engine running. He's getting impatient.

I'm racing to get on board, but I trip on the top step. Going too fast. My bag thumps on the floor and everything spills into the aisle. The door thwacks shut behind me. Mr Greenwood speeds round the corner. The bus creaks over to one side. It feels as if its wheels are going off down the road on their own. I hang on tight with one hand and try to scoop my stuff back with the other.

I get most of it into my bag, my bag onto my shoulder and stand up to go to my seat. That's when the horns start blasting.

'Watch out!'

'Stupid idiot.'

'Want to get yourself killed?'

I'm flung sideways as a high school kid steps out into the road without looking. The bus clanks to a halt and I land half on, half off Enya's lap.

I groan.

Some moron in the bus starts giggling. Then they all start.

'Shut up!' I yell.

I wait for Enya to protest. It's the least she can do. She complains, I shout back. That's the way it should be. That's what I'd do.

But she doesn't. She just picks up the book that I've knocked out of her hand and keeps reading, without saying a word.

I sit down in the empty seat.

The high school kids get on the bus. They all have their own seats. Sometimes we pretend we're big time and sit in them for the short trip from our school to theirs. We say we'll stay there all the way home, but once the big kids get on, we never do.

My two sisters get on. As soon as they sit down, Lizzy leans over and starts whispering to them. She needn't bother. I can hear what she says about me. Pip just ignores her, but Chari gives one of her dramatic sighs.

'Not again,' she says. It's embarrassing for her, having me for a brother.

Chapter 2

At home we dump our schoolbags in our rooms. Mum has a fit if she finds them any-where else. Then we all end up in the kitchen, making our after-school snacks.

'Who's that new girl, Tas?' Chari wants to know.

I'm busy concentrating on not spilling my Milo, so she waits till I sit down then leans towards me.

'The new girl?' She's talking to me two centimetres from my face, as if I'm deaf. '. . . at your school?'

I shrug my shoulders.

'Come on, Tas.' Pip gets in on the act. 'You sat next to her on the bus. What's her name?'

'Enya.'

'Funny name,' Chari says. 'She talks funny, too.'

'That's because she comes from Northern Ireland. Where they have all the bombs and stuff.'

'Ahh.' Mum comes in with a load of washing off the clothesline and upends the basket on the cane armchair. 'I wondered if those new people had any children. They've moved into the old house on Ruddocks' place.' Mum knows all the goss.

'She gets on the bus before us,' Pip says, confirming what Mum thinks. We've always been first on, last off the school bus, because the Ruddocks' kids have all grown up.

'What's she like?' Mum wants to know.

'She has this lovely, white skin,' Chari says enviously. 'And long black hair. Like Snow White.'

'She can't have been in Australia long, then,' Mum says quickly, so that Chari doesn't start going on about her own red frizz and freckles again. 'By the way, whose turn was it to do the chooks today?'

'Mine,' I say.

'They're all in my garden again! Thomas, I wish you'd be more careful. I warned you yesterday about that gate.'

'I *was* careful. I made sure the latch was closed.'

Mum sighs. 'Just go and get them in. And

make sure you get them all. We don't want to lose any more.'

No use arguing with Mum when she uses *that* voice. I try looking hurt and innocent instead. That makes Chari mad. She reckons I only have to put on my choirboy look and people forgive me anything. She's just jealous.

'Go on,' she says, giving me a shove towards the door.

I whistle up Reebok to help me get the chooks in. That's Reebok the Runner. He's our sheepdog. He is very conscientious about rounding things up. Sheep. Chooks. Travelling salesmen. One day we came back from town and Reebok had the stock agent cornered in the sheep yards. The poor bloke must have been there for hours. He'd almost lost his voice.

'G-g-get him off me,' he said, in this hoarse sort of whisper. He never came back, that bloke. They sent a different rep after that.

'Reebok! Here boy.'

We've always been mates, Reebok and me. Mum says he has saved my life at least once that she knows of. She says that, when I was little, I got through the fence into the paddock where the bull was. We had this really stroppy old bull for a while. He used to stamp and snort and paw the ground all the time. Anyway, there I was with the bull charging at me and Mum racing out from the house and Reebok did this flying leap. Landed right on my chest and knocked me out of the way. The bull went charging past. His hoof whacked me on the side of the head. By the time Mum got to me I was bawling my eyes out. And Reebok was so pleased with himself he was running in circles around us both. All the doctors said I was lucky to be alive. That was the good news.

Now Reebok is running in circles around the chooks. I hold the gate open and stand back, so I don't block their way. He sends them scuttling in, all flustered and squarking. Their feathers tickle his nose. 'Chew ... snuffle ... chew.' I laugh at him, so he comes snuffling up for a fight. We race back to the patch of lawn under the clothesline. I fling my arms around his neck and he rolls me over and over. He's all wiry muscles, soft ears and wet tongue. He keeps trying to sit on me, but that would mean he wins, so I struggle to stay on top. When we're both puffed out we lie on the grass together and Reebok licks me wherever his tongue can reach.

On my way back to the kitchen I hear Mum say, 'Are they being mean to Thomas?'

I hate it when they talk about me. No one

else knows what it's like to be me. And Chari always dobs. So I head for my hide-out. It's right under the kitchen. I can hear everything from here.

'But Mum, he just doesn't think. He doesn't care *how* he looks – or *what* other people must think of us. He's *so-o gross*!' Chari says in her drama-queen voice.

'But surely it was an accident,' Mum says.

'An *accident*! Lizzy said he was fighting with Dreadlock *again* and being really *dumb*. Everyone was fed up with him. Mr Greenwood had the engine running and *everything*!'

'I wish he would stay away from Darren,' Mum says. 'What about his other friends?'

'Skip and Bennie?'

'Yes. They seemed much nicer.'

'They're trying out for the junior footy team in town, now. With Dreadlock. They think they're big time. Always showing off their "moves". Very macho,' Chari says sarcastically.

'Oh.' There's a pause. 'When Thomas was younger he seemed to make friends easily,' Mum says.

'He was sort of cute, then,' Pip says.

'Yeah, now he's just a *grot*,' Chari complains.

'You *do* have to make allowances, dear.'

Chari gives a long, drawn-out groan. 'Make allowances! For that little toad! He gets away with murder as it is. Why couldn't we just live in town? Then I wouldn't have to go to school on the bus with my der-brain brother and all those other snotty little kids.'

'And why wasn't *I* born in a palace with loads of servants?' Pip says in a pained voice, taking Chari off. 'Then *I* could have a governess all to myself and *I* wouldn't have to go to school at all.'

Mum laughs. 'And why didn't *I* marry an incredibly wealthy sultan with half a dozen lesser wives to do the work *and* look after the grizzling children?'

Then Pip says, 'Let's get her, Mum,' and they chase Chari around the table. Their feet perform a dance above my head. Mum's hard leather heels tapping out the beat while the girls' runners swish and squeak as they stop and turn.

'Got ya!' Pip laughs triumphantly.

'Beg for mercy!' Mum tickles Chari who laughs and splutters.

'No!'

'Yes!'

'No!' They all flop down, exhausted. The legs of their chairs scrape on the floor tiles.

'Go on. Off you go and do your homework,' Mum says when she's got her breath back.

'I did it on the bus,' Chari says.

'Well go and help your father. He's sorting the sheep for crutching.'

I stay in the hide-out for a while, thinking about Pip's palace and Mum's wealthy sultan. I wouldn't really want to swap with them. And I would *hate* to live in town. I know every tree and rock and fencepost out here.

No one else knows about my special place under the high side of the house. Only Reebok. And even if they do find out, they're all too big to get in here. Except Chari, maybe. But she'd never come in this far. She's scared of the dark. So is Pip. But I'm not.

Just as well I'm not fat. At school I hate being the smallest, and the youngest, and the skinniest kid in the class. But if I was any fatter, I wouldn't be able to get in here. It's a bit tight, wriggling through the wooden stumps and the crossbars that hold the house up. But once I'm in, it's great – cool and dark and secret. I can do whatever I want to do. Be whatever I want to be.

There's a car coming up our road. I wonder who it is. Sounds like Granny Anne. You can practically hear her old Volkswagen coming before she leaves home. Reebok and I scramble out to meet her.

'Hello, Tas. Hello, Reebok. Hey, don't bowl

me over, you two. Have a little respect for your aged granny.'

'You're not an aged granny,' I say.

'Charming child,' she says, and ruffles my hair with one hand as we walk up to the house together.

Mum meets us at the door.

'Hello, Mum.' Granny Anne is my mother's mother.

'Hello, dear. I brought you some grapefruit for your marmalade. The fruit is just *dripping* off my tree at the moment.'

We all go inside. Mum and Granny Anne chat away. I hang around because I like talking to Granny Anne. And I know they'll have a cup of tea and some of the cake that Mum made this morning. I want to be around for the pickings.

'Where are the girls?' Granny Anne asks.

'Charlotte is out helping Denton.' That's my dad. 'And Phillipa is doing her homework, I think.' Mum is the only person in the world who always calls us by our full names. Still, if you are married to someone called Denton, you can't really call him 'Dent'. It makes him sound like a beat-up Holden or something.

I eat two pieces of cake in record time and try for a third while Mum is busy over at the stove, refilling the teapot.

'Uh, uh,' she says. 'No more, young man.' I swear she's got eyes in the back of her head. Then Granny Anne distracts her.

'Oh, Tas. I nearly forgot. I was cleaning out the last of your grandfather's things and I found his mouth organ.' She digs around in her bag. 'Remember those lovely sing-a-longs we used to have?' Her voice goes all soft and dreamy. 'You on the piano, Helen. Your father playing the mouth organ. Everyone singing. It's such a pity you didn't keep up your piano playing, dear.'

'Mum!' It's an old argument. Granny Anne says Mum gave up a promising career as a concert pianist to marry Dad. 'You know I can't possibly fit a piano in this house,' Mum says wearily. 'And when would I get the time to play it?'

'I just think it's a pity that the children are missing out,' Granny Anne goes on.

'Look, we went through all that with the girls,' Mum says. 'They nagged me to let them learn, then they lost interest after the first few months. I know Thomas amuses himself on your piano for hours . . .'

'He does more than that, dear. He invents his own tunes, with wonderful harmonies. He's very good.'

'Well, anyway, it's just too much. Running

in to town all the time to pick them up from piano lessons. Then finding time for them to do their practice.'

Granny Anne sighs. 'The world moves so fast nowadays. There's no time for anything.'

She gives the mouth organ to me. First I blow the wrong side.

'Other way,' Mum says. So I turn it around. It makes the most beautiful bubbly sound. Like water running over rocks. I blow the notes from low to high, high to low. I can feel something inside me rising, sort of expanding. A funny feeling. Light and exciting.

I blow a few more notes. Maybe it will make a tune for me. It's messy at first. Not really a tune at all. But then it starts to come. Pah, pa pa pah, pah paaah.

Granny Anne applauds. 'I told you the boy has talent,' she says. 'He has always had such a good ear for music.'

'Mmm.' Mum is busy finding enough potatoes for dinner.

Chapter 3

I don't like new kids coming to school. I just get everything under control and some new kid arrives. It takes ages to sort them out sometimes, to make sure they know what's what.

First I try my stumble-bum technique. Dreadlock falls for that every time, but of course he would. It works best in Art when there's paint and glue and stuff everywhere. I just pick my time to go to the clean-up sink and knock into something. If I'm lucky, there's a chain reaction and two or three things go over at once. You should hear Dreadlock raising the roof. He's always loudest.

'He did that on purpose, Mr Mac.'

But I act all innocent and he can't prove a thing.

Doesn't work with Enya, though. When I knock the paint all over her work, she just gives this strangled little gasp and goes very quiet. I have to admit I feel a bit mean.

So I try a different approach. Sitting in her seat, right on the siren, going through her desk tray so she'll be sure to see me. She doesn't say a word. Just sits in my seat and goes through my tray. Cool or what?

We're making these sock puppets for the play we're putting on at the assembly. We've got heaps of bits and pieces that Old Mac's collected. Like fur and leather and silky stuff and felt. I get the longest sock in the bag. I find some wobbly plastic eyes in a container on the art trolley. I pull the backing strip off the wobbly eyes and stick them on the sock. They make these faint, clicking sounds as they roll around on the face. Now it needs some teeth.

But the siren blares. It's lunch-time. Everyone's supposed to go out to the lunch area.

'Aww!' There's a chorus of voices.

'Can I just put this hair on, Sir?'

'And me, too. I've nearly finished mine.'

Mr Mac is so surprised that anyone would want to stay in at lunch-time that he lets us.

I glue a long piece of felt into my puppet's mouth, for the tongue. Then I start clowning around with a puppet on each arm, making this ga ga sort of voice. I can do voices. The other kids laugh so I do it some more. Dreadlock says, 'Hey, this one looks just like Miss Watson with that fur on top of its head.' So I use Old Mac's voice for one and Miss Watson's voice for the other.

    Mac: 'Darlene, you have the cutest turned up nose.'

Watson: 'Oh, John, I go weak at the knees when you look at me with those wobbly eyes.'

    Mac: 'And your hair, it's so ... so ...'

'Moth-eaten,' one of the audience interjects. Everyone falls about laughing.

Watson: 'Oh, John, what strong hands you have.'

    Mac: 'All the better to grope you with, my dear.'

Laughter. Then a sudden hush.

I realise, too late, that it can mean only one thing. My leering Mr Mac puppet is already planting the noisiest, most passionate kiss on the simpering Miss Watson. Of course the audience has melted away like ice-cream in a heatwave, leaving me crouched behind the makeshift puppet theatre with two anything-but-innocent puppets on my hands.

'Quite a performance, Tas. Not in the best

of taste, but very much what I have come to expect from you recently.'

I open my mouth, but another voice is answering.

'It was only in fun, Sir.'

I can hardly believe my ears. Enya has not melted away with the others.

'I realise that, Enya. I know you meant no harm, Tas. But that doesn't mean that no harm has been done. Now, out you go, both of you. This classroom is out of bounds at lunch-time.'

I open my mouth to remind him that he gave us permission to be there in the first place, but Enya drags me out by the hand. When we're well away from the classroom I say to Enya, 'Why didn't you run off, like the rest of them?'

She is quiet for a minute. She takes her own time to do things.

'It didn't seem fair,' she says at last.

We go over to the monkey bars and swing for a while.

Ruddocks' old house is only two kilometres away from ours. Enya starts riding her bike over here after school sometimes. We mess about on the tyre swing and the old machinery. There's an ancient plough, near the shed.

It has two seed boxes that we can climb right into. We send messages to each other, in code, through the dividing wall.

If the tractor is in the shed, we pretend it's an army tank and go off delivering aid to Sarajevo. I want to mount machine guns on it, to wipe out the resistance fighters. But Enya won't have a bar of it. She hates guns.

'I bet it was exciting, in Northern Ireland. Living so close to all that action. Like in the movies,' I say.

She gets mad, then. Her accent is much stronger when she's mad.

'Tas, you d' not know what you're sayin'. Real people are gettin' killed. Our own people.'

It's the only thing that really gets her going.

When it's hot we go down to the creek and swim. Then we sit on the bank, talking, drying off.

'Do you miss it?' I ask.

'What?'

'Ireland. You know. Making snowmen, going skating, riding toboggans and all that.'

'Snow is horrible, slushy, slippery stuff to be out in,' she says. 'But I do miss the people. In the city there were always people visitin', callin' by – y' know.'

'My cousins live in the city. But I hate it.'

'Why?'

'All that noise. And the smell of the traffic. And everyone having to be somewhere else – ten minutes ago. It sort of squashes me. Anyway, I like it here. I never want to live anywhere else.'

'Never? Never ever? Even when you grow up?'

'I'm not going to grow up. I like the way I am.'

'But that's daft. Everybody grows up. You can't just stop.'

'Why not? Granny Anne says you're only as old as you feel. Last year, on my birthday, I didn't feel any older.'

Enya sits quietly under the big, shady tree, thinking about it.

After a while the kookaburras and silvereyes forget we're there and come back to perch in the tree and sing. Enya sings too. Irish rebel songs. Folk songs. Some of them I've heard before, so I try to play them on my mouth organ. Enya doesn't seem to notice if I make mistakes. She just keeps singing.

Some days we stay in the house. I have my own CD player in my room now. Mum got sick of me playing the one in the lounge-room all the time. Reckoned I was wearing it out. So they bought me one for my birthday.

'We had to leave all our tapes and CDs behind,' Enya says.

'But you've bought new ones.'

'No. We can't afford to. Anyway, we haven't got a player any more.'

I don't know what to say. Leaving your friends and the places you know would be bad enough, but not having any music! I try to imagine what it would be like. Then I put on the Fifth Symphony – very loud.

It's powerful stuff. It shuts out everything. Then, after a while, it brings the world back down to a size that I can cope with.

By the end of the first track it has also brought Pip out of the shower.

'Turn it down!' she yells from the doorway. 'See those cracks in the wall,' she says to Enya. 'Tas's music causes more structural damage around here than a tropical cyclone.'

'You can talk,' I say, turning it down a fraction so that she can hear me. 'What about your video hits show on TV?'

'At least that's decent music,' she says, and flicks her wet towel at me. I dive for her ankles, but she gets away. So Enya and I stretch out on the cool floor and listen to the rest of the symphony.

When the wild blackberries that grow along

the creek are ripe, we all go down after school to pick them. Pip and Chari like Enya too, even though she's younger than them. They can't understand how a nice girl like her can be friends with a goofball like me. They don't say it, because they know I'd sock them one. But I know that's what they think.

We pick a plastic bag full of blackberries for Mum and about half a bag for us. Then we sit in the shade with our feet in the water and eat them. They're plump and sweet and juicy.

When we've all got our mouths stuffed with blackberries, it's so quiet. The bush ticks with late afternoon sounds. The silver-eyes twit to each other and a bullfrog adds his double-bass voice to the chorus.

That gives me an idea.

'Hey, that frog is just what I need.' I stop myself just in time. 'For our science table at school,' I lie. Pip and Chari are anything but enthusiastic.

'Yuck.'

'No, seriously. I need to win a few points with Old Mac and we're doing this thing on amphibians – aren't we Enya.'

'Yes. Good thinking, Tas. All we have to do is catch it.'

'Reebok will help. Won't you boy?'

'Great help he'll be,' Pip says. 'He'll go

blundering in and the frog will dive straight into the creek.'

We move slowly, so as not to frighten the frog. I hold Reebok's collar so he doesn't get excited and jump in too soon. His tail is going a hundred ks an hour and he's trembling all over. We empty the last of the blackberries all into one plastic bag and Enya holds the other one ready.

The frog just sits there, in the mud. Not croaking now, but making very faint little gulping sounds every three seconds. Enya creeps up one side. Reebok and I are on the other.

'Got 'im,' she says. 'Oops. No. Grab him, Chari! Look! He's just there.'

'No way!' Chari jumps back.

Enya lunges at the frog and slips in the shallow water. But she's caught it.

'Quick, Tas. Hold the bag.'

Between us we get him in. He is *not* impressed and puffs himself up. But we tie the top of the bag and he's in a sort of balloon.

'Should we put in some grass, or something?' Enya says. 'For him to eat.'

'Frogs don't eat grass,' I tell her.

'That's right. Insects then. And a bit of water to make him feel at home.'

We have a discussion and decide that he'll

be okay in there until we get back to our house. Then we'll put him in an ice-cream container with water and rocks and stuff.

'Mum where's a lid for this ice-cream container?'

'Aren't there any in the cupboard, under the sink?'

'No.'

'Well, I don't know. Have you and Reebok been using them as frisbees again?'

'We have ... but ...' It's a great game. I send the plastic lid spinning out as far as I can and Reebok brings it back for me to throw again. Sometimes he gets a bit distracted and goes off chasing a rabbit scent. And sometimes my arm gets tired and we roll on the grass instead.

'There's one on the roof,' Chari says. She is still finishing her breakfast.

'Great.'

'Thomas, you are not climbing on the roof.'

'No, Mum. But if Chari tells me whereabouts on the roof, I can knock it down with that long-handled paint-roller thing.'

'What do you want the lid for anyway?' Mum says.

'To take the frog to school.'

'Can't you just put cling-wrap or something

over the container? You could hold it on with a rubber band.'

'Good idea.'

Mum hands me a big rubber band and the cling-wrap she has been using to package all the lunches.

The bus gets to school any old time. Some days quite early. Some days really late, if the roads are wet or Mr Greenwood starts gasbagging to any of the parents who are dropping their kids at the bus stop.

Thank goodness he's early today and Miss Watson is not in her classroom yet. I go in the back way, through the wet area, so no one in the other classroom will see me.

I open the drawer of Miss Watson's desk, move the stapler and the two-hole punch back a bit to make room, put the frog in and push the drawer shut quickly.

I wonder if she will go to her drawer before all the kids are in the room. But I think it's not likely. She and Mr Mac work and chat in the staffroom before school, and don't usually go to their own rooms till the siren goes.

Now all I have to do is hide in the toilet till everyone goes in, then think of some excuse to knock on her door.

When the din has died down and the chairs

have stopped scraping, I go round the pathway outside her room. Confident walk. Serious look. As if I've been sent on an errand. I knock on Miss Watson's door.

'Yes, Thomas.'

Rats. She remembers who I am. Oh, well, here goes.

'Excuse me, Miss Watson, Mr McKinlay's stapler has disappeared again and could he please borrow yours for a few minutes?'

'Hob-goblins been visiting, have they? Well, see that mine doesn't go missing as well.' She moves towards her desk. I try to breathe evenly. She opens the drawer.

Then the calm is shattered. Miss Watson lets out a shriek. Kids leap up. Chairs fall back. Some kids shout, 'Grab it!'

Others screech, 'Get it away from me!'

'Where did it come from?'

'How did it get here?'

I turn my head to hide the grin on my face, and make myself scarce.

'You're late again, Tas. What is it this time?' Mr Mac sighs.

'Didn't hear the siren, Mr McKinlay. Must have a bit of a cold. My ears are blocked.'

He's sort of given up on me.

By recess time the frog has been caught and

the kids from Miss Watson's room have donated it to Mr Mac for our amphibian project.

'Tas, what happened to that frog we found in your creek?' Enya and I are out in the playground finding a couple of large rocks to put in the aquarium for the frog to stand on.

'Well,' I say, 'I was carrying it across the playground this morning and I dropped the ice-cream container. The cling-wrap came off and the frog got away.'

If Enya has any suspicions, she is keeping them to herself.

Chapter 4

At the end of March we get a burst of hot weather. Summer is not giving way to autumn without a fight. After an hour on the bus in the afternoon, I could win an Oscar for my wilted-lettuce impersonation.

I'm in the kitchen, putting ice into my cold drink, when Enya arrives on her bike. I get out another glass, put in two ice cubes and hand her the orange juice. She pours, and drinks quickly.

'They're having a blizzard in Belfast,' she says, after she has drained her glass and is sucking on the ice cubes. 'We heard it on the news.'

'Half their luck,' I say. Then I call out to Mum. 'We're going for a swim,' I shout.

'Okay, Thomas.' Mum's voice comes drifting down the passage from one of the front rooms. 'Don't forget your hat.'

We go down to the river. But the water in the pool near our house has almost gone. Maybe the big pool further upstream will be better. It's usually the last one to dry up.

Reebok goes charging ahead of us, snuffling in under bushes and crackling through the dead leaves.

The sun burns fiercely as we leave the ploughed firebreak and go through the fence to the water's edge. I haven't been here since last summer.

'Hey, this is great!' Enya suddenly rushes ahead. 'You didn't tell me there was a rope swing here, Tas.'

'There wasn't – last year.'

'Well there is now.'

We stand under the big river gum that hangs half its branches out over the water. Enya gives the rope a few tugs to make sure it's firmly tied on.

'Stand back, Tas,' she says. 'You might get hit there.' I go and stand with my back against the tree trunk. Even there I can feel the swish of air as she swings past me and out over the water.

'Wheeeee ...' Her voice swings out and away until it is lost in the watery whump and splash as her body enters the pool.

'That was fantastic,' she calls as she swims back to shore. 'I'm going again.'

'How deep is it?' I try to imagine the sensation of flying through the air then plummeting into the water.

'I touched the bottom with my feet,' Enya says. 'Have a go.' She climbs out onto the bank, water streaming off her. 'Come on.'

I hesitate.

'Come on. You can do it,' she says. I'm used to people telling me *not* to do things. That it's too difficult, or dangerous, or maybe I should wait till I'm older. The butterflies are going berserk in my stomach, but I hear myself say, 'Hold the rope for me.'

She grabs the loose end of the rope and passes it to me. Drops of water from her hair spray onto my hot skin. They feel wonderfully cool. What will it be like? Swinging on the end of that rope? Flying through the air and landing in the cool water? I remember the rush of wind as a mopoke flew out of the machinery shed one day, right past my head. I have to try it.

'Stand here,' Enya says. 'Reach up and grab the rope – then swing. It's easy.'

I catch hold of the rope as high up as I can and lift my feet. But I only swing a little way and land on my bottom on the bank.

'You have to run with it. Like this.' Enya catches the rope as it swings above me, pulls it with her up the bank, then runs. 'Lift your feet up after the first few steps and swing.' She laughs and splutters, and disappears under the water again. Then she clambers out onto the bank and hands me the rope.

I pull it as far up the bank as it will reach.

'Go, Tas. Go now!' Enya yells.

'Watch out,' I call, my heart pumping wildly. I run, jump, fly through the air, holding my breath. Splash! The water is cold as I go down, down, down. I'm going to drown. My lungs are bursting. Then my feet hit the bottom and I push up again. My head breaks the surface. I gulp in some air and shout, 'Wahoo.'

I did it!

We have about a dozen turns each. The sandy surface of the bank where we take our run-up is getting scuffed and churned up. After a while, Reebok gets tired of rushing back and forth, barking at us. He flops down beside the tree, panting. Then he starts to dig a hole. He does that sometimes, when he wants to cool off.

As I do my next run up, I feel my toe scrape against something hard. Must be a rock under the surface. I can't stop. I fly out on the end of the rope and free-fall into the water. When I reach the bank again Enya is kneeling beside Reebok, scraping away more sand with her hands.

'What is it?'

'It looks like a wooden box,' she says.

'Pirate's treasure?' I say, only half joking. I start digging too. We uncover one of those rope handles on the end of the box. I pull. It's very heavy. Enya pulls too. The box begins to move, sluggishly, out of the hole. As we brush more sand off it, Enya jumps away as if it has burnt her.

'What's wrong?'

'Put it back, Tas,' she says urgently.

'Why?'

'I just have a feeling about it.'

'What feeling?'

'It scares me.'

'Don't be stupid. I want to find out what's in it. And who put it here. And why.'

Her voice goes very quiet. 'I think I know what's in it.'

'How do you know?'

'Just put it back, Tas. Please.'

'No way.' I've almost got it open. The top is nailed down, but one of the boards is loose enough for me to get my fingers under it. 'I need a rock, or something. A flat one.' I search around and find a strong stick. But it breaks when I try to raise the lid with it.

'I have to go home now.' Enya is moving away from the box as if it's alive.

'Wait. Don't you want to see what's in it?'

'Please, Tas, Don't mess with it. It ... it looks dangerous.'

'Dangerous! How?'

'Like it might have bullets in it.'

'Bullets!'

'Yes. I've seen boxes like that. They have bullets in them.'

'But this one can't possibly have bullets in. Can it?' The idea is so way-out it takes a few seconds to register. 'Who would bury *bullets*? Here?'

'Come on, Tas. Let's just put it back and go. Whoever buried it might come back.'

'No. I want to make sure.'

Enya starts to shove the box, pushing it back into the hole. But I pull against her. Hard. As we struggle, the loose board comes off the top.

'It smells like fertiliser!' I'm really disappointed. But the next moment my exploring fingers touch the cold smooth hardness of metal.

Enya just sits there, silently.

I run my hand along the tight-packed row

of bullets lying in the box. Like running your fingers over corrugated tin. 'They're like the bullets for Dad's .22, only bigger,' I say. 'But where's the gun?' I lift out one of the round, blunt missiles, expecting another row of bullets underneath. Instead I find a plastic bag.

'What's this?' I pull it out. The row of bullets rattles and some fall into the hole left by the bag. 'It *is* fertiliser.' I bring it up close to my face to check.

'Fer the Dear's sake will y' put it back, Tas!' Enya tries to take it from me. I snatch it back. 'It's no' fertiliser. It's fer makin' bombs!'

'Bombs! How do you know?'

Her voice drops to a whisper. 'My uncle hid some in our back garden once – in Belfast. Mam was ragin' fit to kill him. We had to leave Ireland after that.'

'You mean this stuff could explode? Kill people?'

'Yes!' Her voice is rising sharply. 'Put it *back*, Tas!'

'But we should tell someone.'

'No!' I'm startled by her fierceness. 'No. You must promise to tell no one. No one. D' y' hear!'

Chapter 5

The temperature has been thirty-one degrees overnight. I haven't slept much. Can't seem to get comfortable. I don't know whether it's the heat, or the thought of those explosives, lying there in their box by the river. Hiding, waiting. But why? How?

Enya has made me promise not to tell anyone. She reckons it's just left over from the war, or something. And it's our secret treasure. I promised – this afternoon. But now, in the middle of the night, I wish I had told Dad. Or Mum.

Who would bury that sort of stuff on *our* farm? It could be left over from the war, I suppose. On the news once I heard about some kids who found an old landmine. The bomb demolition squad had to come and set it off. Right there. Where they found it. That would be cool fun. I bet they'd hear the explosion all the way to Frankstone.

But the bullets belong to a gun. The gun might belong to a murderer. Or a robber. What if they've killed someone? What if they come here and try to kill us! Maybe someone was hiding nearby and saw me and Enya find the box. They'll come after us for sure. I wish I'd told Dad. Should I wake him up now? No, better not. I'll tell him first thing in the morning.

Suddenly Mum is shaking me.

'Thomas! It's late. The alarm didn't go off. Quick. Get up or you'll miss the bus!'

When I get to school Dreadlock comes up to me and says, 'Hey, Tas, I've got this really interesting flower here. Smell this.'

Of course I'm not expecting one of those lapel flowers that squirt you in the eye.

'You creepy slime-bag!' I yell. I feel the anger turn to ice inside me as the water runs down my neck and soaks into my collar. 'You'll be sorry you did that, Dreadlock.'

'Yeah?' he sneers. 'Who'll make me sorry, eh? Not you, you ponsy little nerd.'

'Wanna bet?' I say. 'Just front up at lunchtime. Behind the practice wall. If you're game.' I wish I hadn't used up that whole packet of water bombs I had. But my water-pistol is still in the bottom of my schoolbag. I hope.

'I'm game for anything you can dish out. Aren't we guys?' Dreadlock says.

There's a chorus of yeahs from Todd and Bennie and Skip.

'Have to bring your nursemaids along, do you?' I sneer.

'Don't worry. It will be a fair fight. One on one,' he says.

'Then leave them out of it. Unless you need someone to hold your hand.'

They don't bother to answer as they go off, talking among themselves.

'You're an eejit, Tas Kennedy.' Enya has come from nowhere.

'Dreadlock started it.'

'Yes, and he'll likely finish it – and you.'

My head begins to clear. The icy determination is melting.

'You know he'll bring his gang,' Enya continues. 'And *they* won't stay out of it, no matter what he says.'

She's right, of course. I wish I could be like Enya. Always in control.

'Well I can't pull out now,' I say. But I'm asking myself how I've managed to get into another fight.

The siren sounds for us to go out to lunch. For once I'm in no hurry. I'm sort of hoping

Mr Mac will keep me in for something, but he's in a surprisingly good mood today.

A long visit to the loo is tempting. But I can't bring myself not to show up. It's not that I'm not scared. I am. But there's always this sort of curiosity, egging me on. Pushing me to do things. Just to see what will happen. As if there's a faint chance that I can win for once – against all the odds. It's a sort of huge chocolate bar, dangling in front of me. I know it's just out of reach, but I have to make a grab for it. Anyway, I couldn't stand them crowing about me being chicken. I have to show.

I load my water-pistol as full as it will go. It's a big one. Holds half a litre of water, so it can do some damage. As soon as we're allowed to leave the lunch area, I make my way around the back of the buildings to the brick wall where kids practise tennis and stuff.

No one here. Maybe they forgot, changed their minds.

Then I hear them coming, whispering together, on the other side of the wall.

Blam! I let go a volley of water.

'Aaaargh!'

'Hey!'

'Not fair,' they complain. But they're onto me now and I get the full blast of a can of Coke that they've been shaking up. I empty

41

my pistol, but they're laughing and running away while I stand there with sticky foam all over my face, my neck and my shirt. Oh well, at least it tastes good.

I go to the water fountain and try to wash it off.

Mr Mac is onto us. 'All right. Hand them over,' he says. I had hoped the heat would dry out my shirt before he saw me. I forgot about the stain. 'I've told you before. I will confiscate all weapons and ammunition. Come on. Where are they?'

For a split second I wonder how he knows about the box, buried by the river. But he means the water-pistols, of course.

'Mine's in my bag, Mr Mac.' He'll take it away from me, but I'll ask for it back tomorrow. He'll give me a lecture, but he won't want it cluttering up his drawer any longer than that.

'Well, go and get it, Tas.'

I get up from my seat and head towards the door.

'And you, Darren.'

'I haven't got one,' he says.

'Oh? Then please explain the state of Tas's clothing.'

'Don't know, Mr Mac. He must have

splashed himself when he was getting a drink.'

When I get back to my seat, Enya is seething.

'Wimps,' she fumes in my ear.

'Wha ...' I'm about to defend myself.

'Not you. Darren and his gang. Too spineless to own up. Wriggled out like a bunch of snakes.'

'Low-life reptiles,' I mutter. But my mind is on other things.

When I get home from school, I hear the post-hole digger working not far from the house. Dad is repairing the fence. I change out of my school clothes. Reebok and I walk up the hill to find him.

'Hi, Dad.'

'Hello, Tas. How was school today?'

'Oh, same as usual. Mr Mac took my water-pistol.'

'What was your water-pistol doing at school? You know Mr Mac doesn't allow weapons of any sort.'

'It's only a toy one.'

'The rule is *no weapons*.' He finishes that hole and moves on up the hill, pacing out the distance to the next one. When he rams the digger into the soil again I ask him.

'Dad, could there still be ammunition and

stuff left over from the war?'

He stops digging.

'On the news a while back there was some-thing,' he says. 'I think it was a landmine. It turned up in the city, when a plumber was laying pipes at the back of a house.'

'Could one turn up here?'

'I doubt it, Tas. There were no army units out here. At least none that I know of. Why do you ask?'

'Enya and I found a wooden box, buried by the river. There were bullets in it. And some other stuff.'

'By the river? Where?'

'Where we went swimming yesterday.'

Dad leans close to me and says, 'Are you kidding me, Tas?'

'No, Dad. Honest.' I can feel his eyes looking right inside me.

'You'd better show me then,' he says.

We set off across the paddock and turn to follow the firebreak. The wind has sprung up. It blows my hair across my face. We push through the line of scrub at the usual spot. Reebok runs ahead. A single twenty-eight parrot calls out a warning to anyone who will listen.

The place is easy to find, beside the big tree. The loose sand piles up at the edges of the hole as I dig. It's almost a metre deep before I'm finally convinced.

There's nothing there.

No box. No bullets. No bombs. No sign that anything has ever been there – except a lot of loose ground. The rest of the bank is firm and smoothed out by wind and floods. I'm expecting Dad to be annoyed about me dragging him away from his work for nothing, but he's not. He walks up and down the river bank, then in and out among the bushes.

'Did you kids tie this rope in the tree?' he asks.

'No, Dad. It was already there when we came swimming yesterday.'

'Mmm,' he says. 'Someone tall. Or a very good climber.' He walks up and down. 'And you didn't light a fire, I hope.'

'Course not! I wouldn't light a fire in the bush, in March!'

'I'm pleased to hear it.' He pokes around some more. 'But someone has.'

The dust and ash from a cold campfire begin to fill my nose and mouth as Dad stirs it up with his stick.

'Could be our chook thief,' he says.

'But all that ammo,' I say. 'Just to kill chooks?'

'I was talking about the fire,' Dad says. 'I

45

haven't seen any ammo, or explosives. Are you sure they were here?'

'Positive!' I say. 'Ask Enya.' Then I remember my promise.

'What's wrong?' Dad says.

'I promised not to tell.'

'Well, since there's nothing *to* tell, you haven't really broken your promise. But it is odd. Someone lighting a campfire, here – at this time of year.'

Chapter 6

Mr Mac wants to see me in his office. I got my name in the punishment book three times this week. He is calling Mum and Dad up for a parent interview.

It's Dreadlock's fault. First there's the water fight. Then he snatches my mouth organ and tries to play it. The sounds he makes with it tear my insides to shreds.

'What do you think, Bennie?' he says. 'A bit more practice and I could be really good. Don't you reckon?'

Bennie groans. I grab Dreadlock around the neck. There's a struggle and Miss Watson appears.

'Fighting again, Tas?' she says with a sigh.

'He's got my mouth organ,' I yell, hating the thought of his slobbery mouth all over it.

'Give it back,' Miss Watson says wearily,

writing in the book. Dreadlock shoves it at me and I spend the next half hour getting every last drop of spit out of it.

Then he pinches my hat and won't give it back. *No hat, no outdoor play.* That's a school rule. But they can't seriously expect anyone to stay indoors all day. I'd die of anaemia. '*Cause of death Your Honour? Photosynthetic arrest. Due to total lack of sunshine and fresh air.*' Like those plants we were experimenting with. The ones we shut in the cupboard. They just carked it. You can't blame them. Their lives weren't worth living.

So we're sitting in the principal's office, Mum, Dad, Mr Mac and me. Mr Mac is the principal as well as our teacher.

'We realise that Tas is not the easiest student to have in the class,' Dad says. 'But we've always hoped that the benefits of him being in the local school, with children his own age, would outweigh the problems.'

'That's certainly been my view in the past. But lately ...' Old Mac breaks off to blow his nose. He's had that cold for ages. Maybe he needs a holiday. '... lately I've begun to feel that he's not really being challenged here. It's not that he can't do the work ...'

'We've been very happy with his progress,' Mum says.

'But perhaps it's time to look at some alternatives.'

I know what that means. Special school. In the city. I feel my insides dropping like a lift.

'I had hoped it would not come to this.' Mr Mac's voice is tired. 'We have tried very hard. We can tolerate a certain amount of disruption. But, if things don't improve, I'm afraid I may have to suspend him altogether.'

There's a faint gasp from Mum.

Dad says, 'We understand. And thank you for your patience.'

I'm sitting here, trying to look angelic. Wondering why the glow from my halo isn't dazzling them.

On the way home in the car they're still talking about me as if I'm not there.

'Maybe we should reconsider,' Dad says.

'I'm not going,' I say from the back seat. But they don't hear me.

'Denton, we've been through all this. We kept the girls here because it was easier financially and better for the family. We can't apply one set of rules to them and another to Thomas.'

'But Tas is in a different situation. What is right for one person may be totally wrong for another. Your notion of equality only works if we are all exactly the same – which we're not – and if we all want exactly the same things – which we don't.'

Mum goes quiet. I don't know whether she agrees with him. Or whether she is just planning her next argument.

But I'm not going to any city school. Like Mum says, we've been through all this before. And I won't go! The high school will be bad enough. It's enormous. And full of stairs and doors. I'll be having to ask for help all the time. I'll feel like a moron. But the city! I'd die – like the plant in the cupboard – away from the farm and Mum and Dad and Reebok. I'd even miss my dumb sisters. And Granny Anne. I won't go!

'I'll run away,' I say loudly. 'You'll never see me again!'

Mum turns around in her seat, but she doesn't say anything.

The days are getting shorter, and cooler. I find an old tarpaulin in the garage. It is a ground-sheet, left over from one of our camping trips. But Chari doesn't like camping any more. She's getting too la-de-da, since she's been in high school. And Mum reckons she's getting too old for it. But that's garbage. Granny Anne loves camping and she's much older than Mum.

I drag the tarpaulin into my hide-out under the house. It makes a great floor. And some of the straight beams under there are like narrow shelves. I keep my biscuit tin on one of them. I've put the rest of my Easter eggs in there, so I can eat them slowly. The smooth sweetness of the chocolate coats my whole mouth. I try not to swallow. To make it last as long as I can.

When it's gone, I get out my mouth organ and teach myself to play 'Four Strong Winds'. It's a great song. It's on one of Dad's old CDs.

It sounds pretty awful at first. I hit the wrong note on the word 'high' every time.

Four strong winds that blow lonely,
Seven seas that run high.

I skip over it on the forty-fourth attempt and go on.

All those things that don't change, come what may,
But our good times are all gone,
And it's time for movin' on.
I'll look for you if I'm ever back this way.

No one can hear me way in here. Or if they can, they don't complain. But when I'm not playing, I can hear them in the kitchen.

Our kitchen is like the centre of the universe. All our lives revolve around it. It has an old wooden table. A really long one, where everyone sits to chat and eat and listen. It's where messages are left, and important bills. It's the first place anyone looks when something is lost. Chari was going on about her friend Elena's house again the other day. 'They have a whole new kitchen. They even have a microwave built into the wall. It's fantastic for heating up frozen dinners.'

'Frozen dinners! Yuck!' I told her.

'How do you know they're yuck?' Chari says. 'We never have them.'

'We did so.'

'When?'

'When we stayed at Uncle Gavin's. Mum and me. For my specialist's appointment.'

'Well, trust you not to like them. You're such a stick-in-the-mud. You never want anything to change.'

'So?' I like things to stay the same. I can manage everything and it's ... well ... less hassle.

From here in the hide-out I can hear the phone ringing, the chairs scraping, the people talking. I've got good hearing. Much better than Pip or Chari, even better than Mum and Dad. But not as good as Reebok. He can hear a rabbit sneeze on the other side of tomorrow.

Reebok is a bit wary of the hide-out. Sometimes he'd rather be outside, but he comes in with me. I've laid the tarpaulin so that it goes up at one end now. It makes like a wall, and stops the wind from getting through. I can bring Reebok's mat in here. But it's a bit smelly. So I pinch one of the old grey blankets. Mum will probably never miss it, and Reebok and I can share.

'What are you up to, Tas?'

Uh, oh. Dad has seen me. He's coming back from checking the windmill. He doesn't normally come in from this side of the house. The sheds and yards and everything are on the other side.

'I'm just shaking out this blanket. It's full of dust and stuff from the last time we had a picnic,' I say.

'Ah.' There's a pause while he thinks. He never does anything without thinking, my dad. Eventually he says, 'Go and see if your mother needs anything in town, will you Tas. I'm going in to pick up some windmill parts and you can come with me.'

Mum always needs something from town. Not that she's not a good organiser. But she's always inviting extra people to stay for lunch, morning tea, afternoon tea, dinner. She figures that anyone who has driven this far out is either lost, or dying of dehydration. Visitors never get away from her in under an hour. Sometimes they stay for weeks. Mum collects people, like Chari collects movie-star posters.

'Come on, Tas.' Dad is ready to go. We climb into the front of the ute, Reebok jumps up behind and we bump across the cattle grid. The wind blows a cloud of our own gravel dust across our noses as we stop and turn onto the main road.

'So what's the problem at school, Tas?'

I shrug my shoulders and feel uncomfortable.

'Mr McKinlay says you can do the work all right. You've certainly coped in the past. This is an important year for you. Your last before high school. You should be working hard. Creating a good impression. It will help, you know. You don't want to be labelled a trouble-maker, or a lazy lout. You have to start thinking about your future.'

I don't want to think about the future. Why can't I stay as I am? Why can't everything stay as it is? What sort of future is there, anyway? For someone like me.

A sudden chill comes over me. The sun has gone behind a cloud. Should have worn my tracky daks. Winter is coming.

In town, we pull up at the bottom end of the main street. Frankstone is not a big town. One street of shops, petrol station, police station, footy oval, tennis courts. The hospital up on the hill. And the schools, of course.

Dad and I get out of the ute. Reebok rushes eagerly to the edge of the tray, but Dad tells him to stay. He'll guard it till we come back. Not that anyone would want to steal it. It's about a hundred years old, and nearly as slow as Granny Anne's Volkswagen.

We pick up the windmill parts, the mail and the potatoes for Mum. On the way back to the ute Dad sees one of his mates. He doesn't say much at home, probably can't get a word in. But when he gets with his mates, he's nearly as bad as Mum.

I can hear Reebok getting excited so I go back to the ute.

'Hi, Tas.' It's Enya.

'Hi. What are you doing in town today?'

'And why should I not be in town today? Do you have sole visiting rights to the entire town of Frankstone, Tas Kennedy?'

She's only kidding, so I give her a dig in the ribs and we stand there chatting about this and that, and patting Reebok.

Suddenly this man comes rushing up. There's a bit of a scuffle. He grabs Enya and drags her away. She lets out a little squeak of surprise. Reebok growls in his throat. And I yell at the top of my voice.

'Hey! Let her go.' She's not struggling now.

Just letting this guy kidnap her. I'm angry and scared at the same time. 'Get him, Reebok.' The dog jumps down and is off like a bullet. 'Go get him, boy!'

I'm still yelling when this strangled little voice reaches me. 'He's my father, Tas.'

Everything stops for a full minute. No one is running. No one is talking. It's as if somebody stopped the tape – then started it again.

Dad yells at Reebok, and runs back to the ute. People start talking and walking about.

'Now, calm down, Tas,' he says when he reaches me.

'But he just grabbed her. Dragged her away. She was scared. I could tell.'

'Okay, okay.' Dad calls 'hup' and Reebok jumps in the ute. Then he bundles me into the front and we take off for home.

Once we are clear of the town Dad says, 'Right, what was all that about?'

'Well, Enya and I were just talking and suddenly she was being kidnapped. No wonder she never invites anyone to her house, if that's her father!'

'How do you know she never invites anyone?'

'Because I heard Kristy and her crowd talking about it. Anyway, I'm her best friend and I've never been.'

'She might be shy, or nervous about how you'd behave. In any case, you can't make these judgements about people, Tas, without knowing all the facts. Maybe her father was in a hurry today, or told her to be somewhere else. There are lots of possible reasons. None of which are any business of ours.'

'But he was so rough. He was hurting her. She was scared.'

'Nevertheless, there's no law against a father removing his own daughter from someone's company – no matter how heavy-handedly.'

'And Reebok didn't like him.'

'It was lucky I was close by. If Reebok had attacked him, *we* would be in trouble with the law. Not that I think Reebok would actually attack anyone. He might bale them up, if he could corner them. But he's trained not to attack the sheep.'

'But it's not fair. Enya never causes any trouble. She's the best kid in the school. Why does her own father treat her like that?'

'Very few things in life are fair, my boy.'

If you ask me, nothing is fair.

Chapter 7

Chari was late feeding the chooks today. She sleeps in at the weekend. When she did get around to it, she found another one missing. That's three we've lost now. She blamed me, of course. Said I must have left the gate open again.

But I didn't. I *know* I didn't.

Next time I'll tie the gate up so tight that no one will be able to get in – or out. Except me. I'll use some of that old fishing line that Dad gave me last holidays. It's really tough, that nylon stuff.

'A fox must be getting in,' Mum says. At least she's prepared to give me the benefit of the doubt.

'Yes, but I can't understand why we haven't heard Reebok barking.' Dad is puzzled. 'He's dynamite on foxes. He flushed one out when we were moving the sheep yesterday. Chased it for miles. We could hear him barking all the way.'

'Did he catch it?'

'I don't think so. He didn't bring the carcass back – but it might have been too far for him to carry it. He might have stashed it in the bush somewhere.'

I decide to be helpful.

'I didn't smell fox on him last night,' I say.

'Hmm,' Dad says. 'And you would have if he'd caught it – the way you two roll around together.'

Dad is quiet for a bit. Thinking. Then he takes his windmill parts and disappears.

It's my turn to feed the chooks again. We do turn about – one day each. There are still fourteen chooks. And the rooster. Maybe Reebok did get that fox after all.

I cut off a piece of fishing line and take it with me. When I've finished feeding the chooks this time, I'm going to tie that gate up so tightly that nothing will get in.

The chooks all come, running and cackling and crowding around me until I scatter their pellets on the ground. Then they forget that I'm there and concentrate on their food, with just a few contented bork, bork sounds.

I bend down and go into the low tin shed where they roost for the night. I find four eggs. One is so freshly laid it's still warm from the hen.

That's another strange thing. It usually takes the chooks a few days to get back to laying eggs after they've been stirred up by a fox. This time they seem to be carrying on as if nothing has happened.

Outside the gate I put the eggs down, carefully, where I won't tread on them, and take the piece of fishing line out of my pocket. I click the gate shut, then thread the fishing line through the wire mesh and around the gatepost. I wrap it around three times, just to make sure, and tie it tightly in place.

I go back to the house feeling pleased with myself. As I walk into the warm kitchen, 'Where are the eggs?' Mum says.

'Damn!' I scuttle out into the cold again, to get them.

I wake up suddenly. It's still dark. I've been dreaming. I've just sailed my ship safely into the lagoon when pirate raiders come swarming over the rails. It's a big old sailing ship, like the one in *Peter Pan*. Mr Mac is reading the book to us in class. The original one, not the Disney one. We're doing some media

60

studies and he wants us to compare the book with the movie *Hook*. It's about Peter Pan returning to Neverland as a forty-year-old man. I've been thinking about it a lot. Why would he grow up when he had everything going for him as he was?

Anyway, these pirates are tying me up with fishing line, wrapped around and around, dozens of times. They're going to put me over the side and keel-haul me. I struggle and twist. With a super-human effort I burst free and slash about with my sword to right and left. I slice the hand off the captain. Blood spurts out everywhere, all over the deck, and the pirates lose their footing. They go slipping and sliding over the side, with a bit of help from me. But I wake up before I get to take over the ship.

Reebok shakes himself noisily on the mat beside my bed. I listen. But everything else is quiet. The wind sighs wearily and the night insects sing soft lullabies. Reebok stands, ears pricked, for a few moments, then turns around and settles down on the mat again.

In the morning Chari comes running back from feeding the chooks.

'There's another one gone!' she shouts.

I race out to the chook yard with the others. There must be a hole in the fence somewhere.

Foxes can get through incredibly small openings. I get there just as Dad is saying, 'Who tied this fishing line on the gatepost?'

They'll work it out anyway, so I might as well own up.

'I did.'

'It's been cut!'

'Cut?'

'Yes. With a knife. Or scissors. Our "fox" has cut through this fishing line, opened the gate and helped himself to another one of our chooks!'

A fox that stands as high as me? With scissors? I chuckle as I picture it. But Dad does *not* think it's funny.

Chapter 8

War has been declared on the chook thief. Dad is really mad this time. It usually takes a lot to make Dad mad, but when he is – watch out.

I suggest a rabbit trap, set in the gateway of the chook pen, to catch the thief. Dad says it's tempting, but we could be had up for grievous bodily harm. Then I think of a trip wire across the path (too dangerous); special staining ink on all the chooks (too time-consuming); a car alarm rigged up to the gate (too expensive).

'I'll just have to stay awake and guard them,' Dad says.

The first night Dad takes his rifle and sleeping-bag and watches the chook yard from on top of the hay in the hay shed. Nothing happens.

Nothing happens the next night, either.

Dad is grumpy and light-headed from lack of sleep.

'I think we'll move the chooks into the house for the night. Then I can guard them from the comfort of my own bed,' he says.

Mum is worried that he might not be joking, so she agrees to take a turn.

Like Dad, she settles herself high up in the open-sided hay shed with the rifle, her sleeping-bag, a thermos and the whistle she uses when she umpires the girls' hockey matches.

In the middle of the night the whistle wakes me. I leap out of bed onto the mat. Reebok is not there. I race out the door and crash into Dad.

'Stay inside! All of you!' he shouts, and runs out into the night, with his dressing-gown flapping.

Chari's window is on the chook pen side of the house. Pip and Chari are already leaning out.

'Look at that!'

'Yeah! Just look at Mum go. She's got him!'

'No. His coat's come off.'

'He's down.'

'Oh no, he's up again. And Reebok is no help. He's so excited he doesn't know which way to run!'

'Grab him, Mum!' Pip shouts.

Reebok barks like mad. There are grunts and gasps.

'Rats! He's got away.'

'He's dropped the chook, though.'

Back in the kitchen, huddling close to the fire that Mum has revived, we warm our hands around our mugs of Milo and talk about it – over and over again.

'Who was it?'

'Where did he hide his vehicle?'

'Why is he stealing just one chook at a time?'

'Why didn't Reebok warn us that someone was there?'

'Did Reebok know him? Trust him? Regard him as a friend and not a stranger?'

'But none of our friends would steal chooks.'

'It wasn't someone I know,' Mum says. 'I was close enough to get a good look at him in the moonlight.'

Dad is sitting there, not saying much.

'Did you see him, Denton?'

Dad nods.

'Well?' Mum seems to think that he knows more than he's telling. 'Have you seen him before?'

'Perhaps,' Dad says quietly.

'Where? When? For God's sake! Someone comes onto our property, steals our chooks from under our noses, and you sit there and say "perhaps"!'

Dad gets up and gives Mum a hug.

'You did well, lass. Now I think we should all try and get some sleep.'

'But what if he comes back?' Chari says.

'He won't come back, sweetheart. Rest assured. He won't come back.' Dad has this smooth sort of music in his voice sometimes. He should try being a hypnotist. He'd be good at it.

We all troop off to bed. Reebok plonks himself down on my mat as if nothing has happened. But I lie awake, wondering who Reebok knows, but we don't, and why he didn't even warn us that someone was there. Is he going deaf in his old age?

Back at school on Monday the bush telegraph has been working overtime. Everyone wants to know about our chook thief. They all crowd around.

'Did you call the police?'

'Did he have a gun?'

'A knife?'

'Scissors,' I say.

'Scissors!! Very funny. Ha, ha!'

'No, dinkum. Dad reckons the fishing line was cut with ...' No one wants to listen to a long explanation.

'Wow. Your mum must be pretty brave,' Bennie interrupts. He wants to be friends again.

'And fast!' Skip doesn't want to miss out on anything, either.

'We got broken into a few weeks back.' Reno has been standing there, not saying much. His dad runs the pub. 'Weird sort of stuff was pinched.'

'What sort of stuff, Reno?'

'Potatoes.'

'Potatoes?'

'Yeah. A whole sack full. And some silver.'

'From the till?'

'Not money silver. Knives and a fork and spoon – Mum calls it "the silver". I wish someone would steal the lot. Then Mum wouldn't be saying, "Have you polished the silver this week, Reno?" and I could do something else to earn my pocket money.'

'Like weigh up the spuds!' Reno's brother is in the same class. Had to repeat a year. 'Big deal. I'd rather polish the silver,' he says.

'Anyway, the cops came around every day for a while. But they didn't catch anyone.'

The more I think about it, the more

puzzled I am. A box of explosives buried by the river. A thief who steals a whole sack of spuds, some cutlery, and our chooks. You wouldn't get much on the black market for a chook! I imagine this gangster with a bulge in his trench coat sidling up to Mr Big.

Mr Big shifts his fat cigar to the side of his mouth and says, 'Okay, Gondo, what y' got for me today?'

'You'll be real surprised, Boss.' The boss leans closer and Gondo says, 'Ain't that just bootiful? A gen-u-ine Rhode Island Red.'

'That sure is some surprise, Gondo. Now I'm gonna give you one.' Mr Big removes his cigar and yells. '*Get it outta here*! Before I start orderin' concrete boots – in *your* size.'

Enya is very quiet. Maybe she just can't get a word in. Old Mac is off sick again and we've got this fire-breathing dragon patrolling the aisles to make sure we don't make a sound during creative writing.

'A quiet classroom is a busy classroom,' she keeps harping. How does she expect us to develop colourful and interesting language if we're not allowed to talk?

'Miss?'

'Yes, Tas.'

'Mr McKinlay lets us discuss our story ideas, before we write them down.'

'I don't care what Mr McKinlay does,' she bellows. I swear the windows rattle, even when she's only talking. She could probably shatter a wine glass at a hundred paces. 'When *I* am in charge of this class there will be *no talking.*'

I duck my head. Should have known better. There'd be more stimulating discussion in a morgue.

What a relief to climb onto the bus after school. I plonk myself down in my usual seat. The engine is running and the other kids' voices wash over and around me.

'Move over, Mullins.'

'What did you get for your science project?'

'I got "excellent".'

'Well, I got a merit award for mine.'

The bus begins to move off.

'Hey! Wait! Enya's not here.'

Mr Greenwood stops the bus.

'Well, where is she then? I'll give her two minutes.'

I stick my head out the window and yell at the top of my voice.

'Enya! Hurry up!'

At last she's here. Puffing because she's been running, but with a strange catch in her voice.

'What's wrong, Enya?'

'Nothing.'

I let her get her breath back.

'Are you okay?' It's not like Enya to be late for anything.

'I'm . . .' She's about to say something else, but she changes her mind. 'I'm okay.'

Kids get off the bus in twos and threes as we come to their stops. Maddie and her brother Reagan, then the three Hill girls. Kristy gets off next. Her big brother left school halfway through last year. He works on the farm now.

Kristy leans over me and says to Enya, 'I've got a new saddle. Why don't you come over for a ride? Your mum could bring you and have a cuppa with my mum.'

'Mam can't drive,' Enya says.

'Why not?' says Kristy.

'She's not learned, yet.'

'Oh.' It takes a second or so for this to sink in. 'Well my mum could come and pick you up. I'll ask her.' Kristy is not easily put off.

'Oh no.' Enya's voice is full of alarm. 'No. You can't . . . I mean, I can't . . .'

'It's no trouble,' Kristy says brightly. 'I know Mum won't mind.'

'No. We have . . . a visitor . . . relatives . . . visiting.'

'They could come too. Mum loves to meet

70

new people.' Kristy is gearing up now.

'We can't. Not today ...'

Mr Greenwood calls out. 'Kristy! Are you staying on all night?' And she has to get off.

'Have you?' I say.

'What?'

'Got visitors from Ireland?'

'Sort of.' She's gone very quiet again.

'What do you mean? You have, or you haven't?'

I wait, but she doesn't answer.

'Look,' I say, 'you don't have to tell me. But I'm not going to blab if you do.'

After another silence she speaks so softly even I have to strain to hear her.

'Dad says I'm to stay away from your house.'

'Why?' I'm furious and puzzled and hurt.

'We've an agreement, Mam, Da and me, not to visit wi' people – till it's safe, like.'

'Hunph! We haven't got rabies, you know!'

'Hush, noo. It's not like that.'

I sit silently with my arms folded.

'Please, Tas,' she whispers. 'Mam's a bit para- noid, but it near destroyed her, leavin' Ireland, then Queensland ...'

The bus stops. Pip and Chari pass down the aisle.

'Come on, Tas!'

I stay in my seat. Enya has never mentioned

71

Queensland before. I have to ask her about it. But Mr Greenwood is complaining.

'What's with you lot today? You all like the bus so much you've taken up residence?'

I get off reluctantly.

Chapter 9

When we get home from school the police are there. I go straight to my room, get changed and head for the hide-out. I want some thinking time. Besides, I hate meeting new people. They give me the creeps. I can feel their eyes boring holes in my face, their voices hammering at me.

I whistle and Reebok bounds up. Everyone else is in the house, so I slide under the verandah and into the hide-out. Just as well there's still some chocolate in my biscuit tin. I'm starving.

I settle down with my back against a wooden upright. I'm trying to sort out in my mind what's going on with Enya, but voices keep coming through the floorboards above my head.

'. . . a description of this man.'

It's one of the policemen talking. Mum answers.

'Tall.'

'How tall, Mrs Kennedy?'

'About a hundred and eighty centimetres, maybe a bit more.'

'Hair?'

'Dark. Very dark. And curly. But he had light skin.'

'Is there anything else you can tell me about him?'

There's a pause.

'His face was thin ... bony. What I could see of it. He was wearing this jacket. It came off when I grabbed him.'

'Hmm. A common brand, but might be useful. Forensic can do wonders these days. Now, thin, prominent bones,' the policeman repeats slowly. 'Anything else?'

Mum is silent. Then Dad says, 'Haven't you girls got homework to do?' Pip and Chari protest, but Dad sends them off to their rooms.

Then, after a long pause, Dad's voice. 'I can't be sure. I was much further away than Helen. But I think I've seen him before.'

'Where?' Mum wants to know.

'It's just a feeling, Helen. I could be wrong. I don't want to cause any trouble for the wrong person.'

'But ... if it's the *right* person, I want him caught.'

'Nevertheless, Mrs Kennedy, we do have to be careful. Now, take your time, Mr Kennedy, but tell me everything. Sometimes the smallest detail turns out to be a vital clue.'

'Well ...' There's still a lot of hesitation in Dad's voice. 'He reminded me of a man I saw in town on Saturday. He has a daughter in Tas's class. The girl was talking to Tas and Reebok, and this fellow came along and whisked her away.'

'And who is this person?'

'I've never met him, but I believe the family has moved into Ruddocks' old place. Dunsomething.'

'Dunleavy,' Mum says. 'But Denton, I can't believe ...'

'I said I'm not sure. Perhaps I'm wrong. I don't want to press charges or anything. Just so long as I don't lose any more chooks. Maybe a visit from the law will be enough of a deterrent. You will pay them a visit, won't you, Sergeant?'

'I will. It's an unusual name, Dunleavy. There was a name like that in a report I saw recently. I think it was in Queensland where that huge arsenal of weapons and explosives was found. Some paramilitary group had

75

been arming itself to the teeth.'

I'm listening in the hide-out with my mouth open. Could it be Enya's father? He wouldn't win the Friendly Neighbour of the Year Award. But stockpiling weapons and explosives! Why would he be stealing our chooks, though? And what about Enya? Does she know about it? She *was* a bit funny on the bus today. She acted strangely when we found the box by the river, too. What is going on?

I'm all fired up to tackle Enya about it on the way to school next day, but she doesn't front. Her seat in the bus remains empty. Her desk at school is empty. By the end of Maths I've imagined at least ten terrible things her father has done to her and I'm worried.

Mr Mac is marking the roll.

'Enya Dunleavy not here today?'

'No, Mr Mac.'

That's it. No 'Do you know where she is, Tas?' or 'Does anyone know if she's sick?' Not a word.

Don't they realise? She could be tied up to her bedpost. Locked in the tool shed. Beaten to death, even. Doesn't anybody care?

'It's Mrs Humphries's day today, Mr Mac.' Mrs Humphries is the school secretary.

'I know that, Tas.' Mr Mac is a bit puzzled.

'Maybe Enya's mum has phoned and left a message,' I say. 'Can I go and ask?'

'No, you certainly cannot. You have your own work to do, now kindly get on with it.'

How can I work when I'm so worried? Maybe the police arrested the whole family and are holding them in custody. Who'll bail them out? They don't really know anyone here.

'Haven't you finished that yet, Tas?'

I bang away at my computer keys. But I have no idea which ones I'm striking.

The day crawls by.

Everyone is getting to me. Dreadlock thinks he's smart. Just because Enya's not here to stick up for me. He's hidden my calculator and when I tell him to give it back he says, 'It's right there. Under your nose.'

But it's not. And I know by all the snickering that he's got it. Or he knows where it is.

Old Mac is not a bundle of joy today, either. He's a bit late into class after recess.

'Held up by a parent,' he says.

'Did they want your money or your life?' I say, not too loudly. But he hears.

'Spare us your wit today, please Tas.'

Sometimes I can cheer him up, but not today. And Enya's not here.

'Smart-arse,' Dreadlock whispers.

That's it! He's really asking for it.

'Right, Dreadlock!' I say with all the menace I can put into my voice. I haven't worked out how, yet, but I'll get him.

I eat my lunch with the others. Mr Mac is on duty and it's not a day to be caught out of bounds. I save the cling-wrap from around my sandwiches, smoothing it out, folding it carefully and stowing it in my pocket. As soon as we are allowed to leave the lunch area, I head for the clump of trees on the far side of the playground.

At first I think I'm out of luck, but then I find one. This clump of trees has a neon sign, in dog language, that says Public Toilet. I feel the dog turd carefully with my bare toe. It's just dry enough and still suitably smelly. I pick it up in my square of plastic. Now to get into Dreadlock's bag without him seeing me.

Dreadlock and his mates are kicking the football out on the grass. It's a sunny day after a week of rain, so everyone is making the most of it. I saunter along, keeping clear of the groups of kids, and reach the row of bag hooks. I find my own bag and move it close to Dreadlock's. If anyone comes along I'll say I'm getting my hat. They're very big on protection from UV rays at this school.

So far, so good. This is Dreadlock's bag and

his library record folder is inside. I unwrap the dog turd and slip it in, pressing just enough to make it stick. Now he'll have to spend hours making a new library record. And he'll probably have to wear a peg on his nose all the time he's doing it. I can just hear his mother: 'I'll never get used to what young people wear. First it was rings in their ears. Now it's pegs on their noses.'

Serves him right.

I dump the plastic in the big bin and go into the toilet block. I'm washing my hands when the siren goes.

The day is dragging towards afternoon recess when Mr Mac decides to check all our library record folders to see how much we're reading. Oh no! He never checks them. Well, once a term, maybe. Why today? Of all days!

Kids are all going to their bags or looking in their desks.

'Wait, Dreadlock. I'll get yours for you if you like,' I say.

But he shoves me aside and gets there first.

'What's that smell?' someone says. I didn't think it was that strong, but it's hard for me to judge how well other people smell things.

I put my library record folder on Mr Mac's desk and slink back to my seat, waiting.

Mr Mac goes over to the window and opens

it. 'It's very stuffy in here today,' he says wearily. He goes back to his desk and arrives just as Darren puts his folder down.

'What's that smell?' he asks. Then everything goes out of control.

Dreadlock opens the folder. Groans. And starts throwing up, all over the desk. He's heading for the door when there's an ominous, thudding crash.

A silence hangs over the room. Then the shock waves race through the class. Kids are screaming. Shouting, 'He's dead!' Running outside. Gagging on the smell.

Miss Watson comes in. 'Phone the ambulance, someone. Hurry.'

People are crowding around Miss Watson as she tries to resuscitate Mr Mac. I'm still sitting at my desk. Absolutely numb.

Chapter 10

I've killed him. That's all I can think about. He's dead and it's my fault. My throat has closed over. I can hardly breathe. I want to die too.

Somehow my lungs keep pulling in air. I hear voices. Disjointed. Bits that don't belong.

'... heart trouble ...'

'... still here ...'

'Get him out.'

Then Mrs Humphries takes my hand.

I try telling myself that a dog turd, and a boy throwing up, do not cause an experienced teacher to have a heart attack. In schools, kids are always throwing up, or messing themselves, or bleeding all over the place.

But Mr Mac is old. An old, experienced teacher. With a dicky heart. I wish I'd known he had heart trouble. I just thought he caught the flu a lot.

Anyway, Dreadlock was supposed to find the dog poo in his library folder when he got home.

I should have listened when they went on at me. All that stuff about practical jokes. I wish, I wish, I *wish* I'd listened. I can't tell Mum what I've done. She has had to drive in to town to pick me up. All the bus kids had to ring their parents to come and get them early. They've closed our school for the rest of the day, but the bus has to wait for the high school kids.

'Are you all right, Thomas?' Mum says.

I nod my head. A thick, dark fog has blocked off all my senses. It is smothering me. Seeping into my nose, my ears, my eyes. Taking all the oxygen out of the air.

'It just doesn't seem possible.' Mum is stunned, not quite believing it yet. I wish I could not believe it.

When we get home, I head straight for the hide-out. I get my mouth organ out and play.

Oh Danny boy, the pipes, the pipes are calling,
From glen to glen and down the mountain side.

The words are in my head, but the music goes floating free. It swells up and out like a rising wave, pulling everything with it. Scooping up all my worries, all my guilt. Then sweeping back to crash over me and dump my body on the sand.

The summer's gone and all the leaves are falling,
'Tis you, 'tis you must go and I must bide.

Suddenly I can't bide any longer. I have to go and go and go. Reebok hears the music and comes sniffing in to find me. Now he scrambles out of the hide-out with me. I grab hold of his collar and we set off across the paddock.

I don't care where we're going. I'm just walking, walking. But Reebok goes along the firebreak and through the fence. He's heading for the river.

The sun has lost what little warmth it had. A breeze is sneaking in around my wrists and ankles. The walking is just keeping it at bay. We walk faster, further. Along the river, past the blackberry bushes. The thorns snatch at my jeans.

We reach the fence at the edge of our property. Reebok stops. *Back now?* he says to me. He knows we turn back here.

'No, Reebok. Not yet.'

We go through the fence and he quickens his pace.

There's a strong smell of wood smoke and ash. Like a campfire when you throw water on it. It's the same smell as Dad stirred up with his stick the day we came looking for the ammunition box.

And that other smell. What is it? I begin to feel hungry. Saliva builds up around my tongue. It smells like ... like ... cooked chicken. No wonder Reebok is in a hurry.

We come out of the bushes and on to the bank at the bend in the river. The water is rushing and gurgling along quite fast now – since the rains. Reebok's body tenses. His tail goes up. We both stand still, turning our heads, listening.

'What is it, boy?' I say softly. Reebok's whole body begins to quiver.

'Hello,' I call. There is no answer. Reebok wants to investigate, but I just want to get away from here. I tug at his collar and he turns, reluctantly. I think about home, but we are much closer to Ruddocks' old house, where Enya lives. It would be good to see Enya. Maybe sort things out. I hope her father is not there, though.

We go through Ruddocks' fence and down the firebreak. I tug Reebok into a run and he forgets about whatever is behind us. I wish I could forget things so easily.

Old Mr Ruddock died last year and the farm is leased out. The Dunleavys just live in the house. I never thought about it before, but why *do* they live way out here? They are not working the land or running sheep or cattle, or anything. Why don't they live in town?

This fence goes all the way to the road. The house is down to the left.

Why wasn't Enya at school today? Does she know about Mr Mac? I don't want to tell her. But I don't want anyone else telling her, either. Bad-mouthing me. I'll pretend I don't know anything about the dog turd. But everyone knows about it by now. That sort of news travels like a bushfire around here. Dreadlock will reckon it was me. Well he can't prove it. Nobody can. Just like we can't prove who pinched our chooks. How was I to know about Mr Mac's heart, anyway? No one ever said why he was away so much.

We've been running for ages. I'm out of breath and I've got a pain under my ribs. I make Reebok slow down. The wind is stronger now. Thunder rumbles away behind us. 'Scattered thundery showers,' they said on TV last night. Reebok doesn't like thunder. He's getting nervous.

We come to Ruddocks' driveway. There are no fences on either side, like there are along our driveway. Just a two-wheel track with a hump of grass in the middle. Reebok is pulling hard, towards the house. I'm stumbling, pulling him back, trying to keep up with him. Until he leaps forward and I lose my grip.

'Reebok!' I yell. But the thunder claps right over our heads and he's off like a bullet.

The path to the door of the house is well worn. One of the old wooden steps creaks against its nail as I climb up onto the verandah. There are voices coming from inside. I go to knock on the door, but it is already open.

'I told you I want nothin' to do with it.' It's Mr Dunleavy's voice. I've only heard it once, but I'd know it anywhere.

Then another voice, not quite the same but with the same accent, says, 'Come on, Dermot. There's good money to be made. Y'll get nowhere workin' at odd jobs for a livin'. Come in wi' me and the lads, eh? I can fix it. Y'll not regret it, I promise y'.'

'Get out o' here, Seamus. Take y'r guns and y'r money.' The first voice is low and tight. Every word clipped out.

'Och, y'r not meanin' that now. I need to lie low for a bit. And you'd not be turnin' y'r own brother away from y'r door. The weather is desperate outside, so it is. And I'm a mite weary o' livin' off the land, campin' out in the cold and the rain.'

'Y're wrong, Seamus. I mean every word. I left Belfast to put all that behind me. I'd a good job in Queensland, until *you* turned up and ruined it. Now I've a new life here. I'll not have y' bringin' the old troubles to me doorstep yet again. I do not know how y' found me, but get out and leave us alone! Y' hear!'

'Sure y' knew I'd find y', sooner or later, Dermot.' The voice is gentle now, persuasive. 'And it's just a wee while I'll be stayin'. Till the heat is off.'

'No! I'll not have you swaggerin' in here wi' your guns and explosives all over me kitchen. I've me family t' think of.'

'And am I not family? Dear God, Dermot, what would our mother say, bless her soul, to hear y' denyin' shelter to one o' y'r own? I promise no one will know I'm here. I won't have to go stealin' me food and drawin' attention to meself if I'm livin' here wi' you, sure I won't.'

There is a moment's silence. I'm standing on the verandah, not knowing what to do. If they find me here they'll know I've heard them. I'm about to sneak away when another voice says, 'Do as he says, Seamus. Get out of this house.' It's a woman's voice, slow and deliberate, but edged with steel.

'No, Mary!' It's Enya's father again. This time there is shock and panic in his voice. 'Put it down! For the Dear's sake!'

Then Enya's voice screaming, 'No! No!'

I'm drawn irresistibly into the doorway. Wanting to help Enya. To stop something terrible from happening. To be on the inside – not outside. Not alone. Feet are scuffling. A chair goes over. Enya is still screaming. Then – bang.

Something hits into me – hard. And all the sound goes dead.

Chapter 11

I'm on my way home. But it seems to be taking for ever. There are people on the track, but they're a long way off. I walk towards them through this bright light. It's like a streak of lightning has been captured in mid-flash and the brightness has stayed, somehow. The light is full of colours. The trees, the sky, the people are all bathed in it. It is so beautiful I just stand there.

There's a house, now, in the distance. The people have gone inside. But I want to stay out here, in the light. They shout and call to me again and again. I'd better go.

I reach the house and go inside. It's dark again. I'm lying in bed. Mum is bending over me.

'Thomas, can you hear me?'

'Mmph.'

'Thank God.' She rests her cheek against mine. I feel her warm tears.

My head hurts. Come to think of it, my arm hurts, and my shoulder. Then I'm trying to find a part of me that feels normal. I have dull aches all over, and a tube attached to my arm.

I have a hundred questions to ask, but I can't stay awake long enough to ask any of them.

I wake up again. This time in a place that is totally dark, totally silent. I move my head carefully from side to side. It feels empty, hollow. Then I hear a voice. It's very familiar. What is it saying? Something, quietly. Then it goes away.

I'm lying in a bed, but it's not my own. Where is everybody? It was so noisy before. Then it hits me. Unless the afterlife smells of disinfectant, I must be in a hospital.

Someone comes padding up to the bed, pauses to check something, and goes away again.

I drift back into a world where nothing is solid, everything is moving – like jelly. Constantly moving. Mr Mac is there. He's leaning over a wavering cliff, looking down. I struggle towards him on a jelly road, springing as I walk, as if I'm on a trampoline. He sees me coming, beckons with his hand. We look down over the cliff together. It's a long way down. And there's black water at the bottom. Then he jumps.

I shout at the top of my lungs. 'No! No! Stop! Come back!' Then I'm falling too. Falling as the sound falls, down, down, down. Falling and getting smaller, further away.

The sound stops. My body jerks to a stop and there are hands on my head, my wrist, my chest. Voices murmur. Something is pressing into my mouth.

'It's all right, Tas. Just breathe in now. Everything is all right.'

The whole family is here. Mum, Dad, Pip, Chari. After the initial greetings no one knows what to say.

I try to speak. I manage to croak, 'What happened?'

There is a pause. Then Dad says, 'You were shot. In the chest. The bullet grazed your lung.' He swallows hard. As if he's trying to talk and eat at the same time. 'But you're going to be okay.'

Mum is crying again. Blowing her nose. 'Yes. Okay,' she says.

I'm trying to put it all together. 'Shot?' I say.

I remember Enya screaming, the loud bang. 'But . . . why . . .? Who?'

'It was an accident,' Mum says. Then, less confidently, 'So they say.'

Then Chari takes up the story. 'There was a lot of blood,' she says enthusiastically. 'Mr Dunleavy used all their towels, and took blankets off their beds. He covered you up while Enya phoned the ambulance.'

Enya's dad? But he hates me. And there was another guy. And someone called Mary. Wasn't there?

'Enya's mum went to pieces completely. Had to be sedated or something. They're all really upset about it. Mr Dunleavy phoned the police himself. Said that the gun went off accidentally – while he was cleaning it – just as you appeared in the doorway. He didn't know you were there.'

Cleaning it? I'm a bit hazy, a bit confused. But I know they were not cleaning that gun. What about the other man? Or did I dream that part? I feel myself drifting off again and struggle to stay awake. Then someone says 'I'm afraid I'll have to ask you to leave now.'

'Not yet,' I try to protest.

But Mum says, 'You must rest, Thomas.'

I'm asleep again before they leave.

Between sleeping and waking and sleeping

again the people come and go. Nurses, doctors, Mum, more nurses and people I don't know. Then Mum and Dad and the girls again.

I try to ask more questions, but they tell me not to think about it. The police have interviewed everyone and they're satisfied it was an accident.

'Is Enya all right?' I ask.

'Everything is all right. You mustn't worry.'

But I am worried. And not only about Enya. No one has mentioned Mr Mac. They must be waiting until I'm stronger. Then they'll charge me with murder. I'll have to stand up in court. In front of everyone. And tell about the dog turd. I'm beginning to wish that the gun had killed me.

Chapter 12

I'm staying awake longer. But the more I stay awake, the more I remember. My brain is telling me things that I don't want to know. Niggling, nagging things. It's telling me they weren't cleaning that gun. And I keep hearing that other voice. A man's voice. A bit like Enya's dad. But it wasn't him. At least I don't think it was. Enya's dad was saying he didn't want any guns in the house. And the other man – his brother? – was asking him to hide them. And talking about stealing food, camping out.

I have no idea which day it is or how long I've been here. Days and nights are much the same in this air conditioning and artificial light. But now that I'm not sleeping so much, I'm beginning to recognise a pattern. There's a long sort of hush, broken by doses of medicine, then breakfast time. A shorter lull to morning tea, then medication again and lunch. After lunch a different lot of nurses come on, visitors arrive, and the place hums with noise and activity until all the visitors leave. Then more medicine and a slow sort of winding down to the swishings and whisperings of the long night.

I'm lying here, dozing, when I hear that voice again.

'Y're Tas, then.'

I don't answer. So many voices have been in my head, this one most of all. I don't think it's real, until suddenly the long curtains sweep around my bed, rattling on their runners. A stabbing pain brings me wide awake. The intravenous drip is ripped out of my arm.

'Pity the wee girl didn't finish you off. Would 'a' saved me doin' it.'

The voice is quiet, not much more than a whisper, but the menace in it sends shock waves of recognition through me. It's the same voice.

'Wh-who are you?' I manage to croak. But already the pillow is being pushed over my face.

'You'll not need to know who I am. Not where you're goin'.'

'But . . .' I struggle. Pushing the suffocating softness away, turning my head.

'You're a snooper,' he says. 'Snoopers are trouble. They know too much. Where I come from they don't survive.'

What's he talking about? I wasn't snooping. I was visiting Enya. This guy is a madman. He can't do this. It's illegal. It's . . . I jerk my head away.

'I don't know . . . anything,' I squeak. But his hand is on my throat, pushing me down and the pillow is clogging all my airways.

I can't breathe. I feel myself drifting, fighting to stay awake, drifting away again. Thoughts fly through my head. Mum, Dad, Reebok. The sun warming my back. The fresh breeze when it finally comes on a summer's night. All the things I'll never get to do again. Like eating the first wild blackberries. Flying like a bird out over the swimming hole. I feel the water closing over my head. The darkness becoming more intense.

Then the unbelievable but unmistakable voice of Mr Mac is saying, 'Hey! What's going on here?'

The pillow falls away. Air rushes into my body again and my brain begins to function.

Mr Mac? But why should I be surprised?

We're both dead, after all. I hadn't expected to meet up with him so soon. Mr Mac examines my neck. It hurts. I thought you couldn't feel anything, once you were dead. But if I'm not dead, then Mr Mac's not either. Slowly an idea is forming in my mind. Is it possible? The ambulance took him away. But sometimes they can revive people.

That's it! It must be. People seem to be coming from everywhere, but I'm only vaguely aware of them. A huge weight is lifting off me. *I haven't killed him! He's alive!* Any remaining doubts are gone when he starts shouting in his playground voice.

'Stop that man!'

'Is the boy all right?'

'He's breathing. Someone get after him! That big bloke ... with the dark hair. He just went out – that way!'

There's noise and confusion and people all around us but I have to try and tell Mr Mac something.

'I didn't mean to ... kill you. I mean ... you're the ... just the best ... um ... teacher, and it was ...'

Then he's laughing. I can't believe it. He laughs like I haven't heard him do for yonks. He sort of collapses in the chair by my bed, still laughing, almost hysterical. Then he stops. 'Sorry,' he says to the nurse who is taking my pulse, attaching the drip tube, wondering what's going on. 'It just seems funny,' Mr Mac explains, 'Tas thinking he's killed me. Both of us ending up in here. I always thought of him as a bit of a terrorist, but never as a danger to my life.' He gives a little left-over laugh, 'h, h, h.'

'In fact, Tas, you probably saved me – saved me from myself, if you like. And it seems I've come along just in time to return the favour.'

I can't let it rest yet. Now that I've started to talk about it, I want to make sure he understands.

'Dread ... I mean Darren was supposed to find it ... at home ... and ...'

'Look. It's okay. What happened to me was going to happen anyway. I've known – and done nothing about it – for a long time. It stopped me in my tracks, but I'll be back at work next term. Right now we have to get to the bottom of this attack on *you*.'

The Head Nurse comes back from wherever she's been and says, 'I'll have to ask you to go back to your own bed now, Mr McKinlay.'

'Yes, Sister,' he says meekly. 'But really, your security leaves a lot to be desired.'

That's more like the Mr Mac I know.

'Maybe so,' the sister says. 'But no one

expects this sort of thing in a quiet town like Frankstone.'

'Indeed we don't,' he says. 'I hope the police have been called.'

'Yes. Rest assured. Everything has been done that can be done. We will make sure that someone stays with Tas, constantly, until this man is caught.'

'Well, in that case I'll say goodnight.' He pats my arm. 'We'll talk again tomorrow, Tas.'

'Goodnight, Mr Mac.'

As he and the sister move away she says, 'It is very unnerving for all of us, but the police will be dealing with it from now on. They want to take a statement from you. We are all very grateful that you were on the spot at the time, but may I ask how you came to be there?'

'I had only just heard about the shooting accident,' he explains.

'If it *was* an accident,' the sister interrupts. 'I'm beginning to have my doubts.'

'Hmm,' Mr Mac continues. 'Tas is one of my students, you know. My own visitors had just left, so I thought I would come and say hello to him. When I saw the curtains around his bed, I almost didn't come into the room. I had, in fact, turned to go, but something . . . I don't know exactly what . . . something made me look again. I saw farm boots. Dirty ones.

Doctors don't usually wear dirty boots – in the hospital. And I heard sounds of a struggle. I sensed that something was wrong.'

'Well, thank you again, Mr McKinlay. If it hadn't been for your prompt actions, well, I just dread to think ...' With that they turn a corner and I lose their voices.

A nurse pulls a visitors chair up beside my bed. 'We've tried to phone your parents, Tas, but they don't seem to be at home.'

'They might have gone to Granny Anne's.'

'We'll keep trying,' she says.

It takes ages, but eventually I fall asleep. In the morning a new policeman comes. They have called for back-up from the city. So we go through it all again. Not that I can tell them much. A man comes, in the night, and tries to strangle and suffocate me. He is big. Well, tall, but bony. One of his hands fits almost right round my throat. And he has an Irish accent. He pulls the curtains around my bed, yanks the drip out of my arm and shoves a pillow over my head.

'What did he say to you?' The policeman is scribbling away on his note pad. 'Try to remember the exact words.'

I try.

The nurses are keeping everything as normal

as possible, but it's not easy when you keep tripping over policemen in your corridor.

Mr Mac comes back to see me.

'Well, Tas, no one could describe your life as uneventful,' he says.

'No.' I shake my head.

He talks about the family and things. Then about school. I still feel terrible about the dog turd.

'It's done, and that's that. We can't go back and undo it.' He goes on talking, almost to himself. 'I used to be able to keep kids' minds occupied with better things. There is so much to learn. You've got a good brain, Tas. You shouldn't waste it.'

'No, Mr Mac,' I mumble. I've heard this before. When adults start telling you you've got a good brain they want you to do something they know you won't like. I know Mr Mac wants me to go away – to this special school. 'I won't cause any more trouble, ever again, I promise. But I'm not going away to school. I couldn't live in the city.'

'Have you ever tried it? Could be great fun. They have wonderful facilities ...' (he means institutions) 'for people ... like you.'

'I'd hate it,' I say through clenched teeth.

'How do you know you would?'

'I wouldn't know where to go, who to talk

to, which bus to catch. There are hundreds of buses in the city, you know. If I got on the wrong one, I might never be seen again. Anyway, I like living here.'

'Resistance to Change,' he mutters. 'Toffler was right,'

'Who?'

'Alvin Toffler. He wrote about the human condition. About how people are afraid of change. Afraid of the unknown. We are all the same, to some degree. But,' he says more positively, 'there's no point in worrying about any of that at the moment. We both have to concentrate on getting well again.'

I hear the lunch trolley clanking in the doorway.

'I'll come and have a chat to you tomorrow,' he says.

'Yes, Mr Mac.'

Chapter 13

Next day I think about avoiding Old Mac, pretending I'm asleep, faking a seizure or something. But I want to get my breakfast in first. Then, before I know it, he's there, sitting in the chair next to my bed. We chat about school again.

'You don't seem to spend so much time with Steve Bennetts and David Skipworth, these days,' Mr Mac says.

'They've got footy training. And they don't want to hang out with girls,' I say. 'But Enya's not like the other girls.'

'Indeed she's not.'

'Anyway, they're in Dreadlock's gang, now.'

'Mmm. Pity,' he says.

Mr Mac is sick of the hospital. He wants to get back to the real world. But, at the same time, he's nervous about it. Maybe he'll retire.

His kids are grown up now. Funny, I never thought about him having kids. Or a wife, for that matter. Mum would say, 'You know Mrs McKinlay, Thomas. She always comes to the school concerts and things.'

I would have to say, 'Yes. I know, Mum.' But I never really thought of them *together*. Old Mac is always the teacher, the principal, the school, almost. Other teachers come and go, but he has always been there.

Mum, Dad, Pip and Chari come in when they can. Pip says the bus ride to school is very quiet without my scintillating conversation. Chari says, 'What conversation?' You have to hit Chari over the head with a joke before she gets it. I can't believe that I actually miss her. In here, there's no one to fight with. Everyone is so polite.

Today they've taken the drip out of my arm and I am allowed to sit up. Mr Mac comes swooping in, just after breakfast, pushing a wheelchair.

'Arise bold Tas, your chariot awaits,' he says.

'Eh?'

'Don't say "eh". Don't they teach you anything at school? I've cleared it with your bodyguard and you and I are going exploring the outer reaches of the universe. We have to be back by morning tea time, though.'

'Great,' I say. To tell the truth, I'm not too sure about it. My shoulder, where the bullet went through, is fine while I lie still. But hurts like hell when I move.

'You've got to wear this sling, to keep your shoulder still,' he says, as if he can read my mind. 'But the outing will do wonders for our claustrophobia.'

Whatever that is, Mr Mac must have it too.

He helps me into the chair. I'm surprised how wobbly my legs are, and they weren't even injured. But we go down the corridor and through the electronic sensor that opens the big double doors.

The air is clean, crisp and delicious. We both drink it in, in huge gulps. Then we go down the ramp and into the garden. It has been raining, but the sun is out now and the smell of the damp soil mixes with the scent of the lavender bushes that stick out over the edge of the path. We brush past them as we clack around on the brick paving. Mr Mac pauses to rest on the wooden bench. It's so good to be out in the open. It makes me feel as if I've just been released from prison. I don't want to go back inside. Mr Mac is not in a hurry, either.

We have three fine days in a row. It's funny that we haven't run out of things to talk about. Sometimes we just sit quietly, soaking up the sun. But there's always more to say. I'm beginning to look forward to him coming each day. It beats being stuck in the ward all the time.

He talks about getting back to school – but I tell him I don't think he should rush it. That gives me an idea. If I miss enough school, I'll have to stay down a year! But that would mean being in the same class as little grommits like Bennie's brother, Ben Two. I don't know if I could stand it.

Mr Mac gets up from the bench where he's been resting.

'Well, we'd better get our exercise,' he says. We do two more laps around the pathway that circles the garden. When we get back Mr Mac is breathing hard. He stops to rest.

'Are you okay?' I ask.

'Yes, yes.' He's irritated. 'Mustn't overdo it, eh?'

The next day is cloudy, but not raining. I suggest going out anyway. Old Mac doesn't take much persuading. This time we set off along the edge of the driveway towards the main gate. It's smoother than the garden path and slightly downhill. A car drives slowly into the car park on the other side of a bushy hedge.

'Who's that?' I'm never sure when Mum or Dad will show up. Because they have to drive so far, the staff let them visit almost any time during the day now.

'It's a pirate raider, sailing into our lagoon,' Mr Mac says. 'Prepare to defend the island.' He pulls up sharply and stands alert and ready.

'Hello,' Dr Ong greets us as he walks over from his car. 'You two seem to be making good progress,' he says. 'Don't overdo it, though.' He goes on into the hospital.

'Phew. I thought he was going to give us a dressing down,' Mr Mac says. 'Capture us and throw us, bound and gagged, below decks.'

We move on down the driveway. The air is warm, but heavy and humid. The sounds of the hospital grow fainter and further away.

There are birds in the trees. Twenty-eights calling out their number on the same three notes over and over. 'Twen-ty-eight, twen-ty-eight.' I take my mouth organ out of my top pocket. I've begun playing it again. I keep it with me all the time now. Its solid shape is familiar and reassuring. I play the same three notes back to the twenty-eights.

Mr Mac stops wheeling my chair.

'Can you play any tunes, Tas?'

'A couple.'

'Come on, then. How about a rousing sea shanty to keep the ship's company working with a will.'

'What's a sea shanty?'

'Dear me, your education has been sadly neglected. I'm afraid I'll have to complain to your teacher.'

This time I grin. He's not a bad bloke – Old Mac.

' "What Shall We Do with a Drunken Sailor". Now that's a good one,' he says.

'How does it go?' I ask.

He starts to sing. We're wheeling slowly down this driveway, Mr Mac singing louder and louder with each verse and me playing. It's a pretty easy tune. By the fifth verse I can even do a fancy trill on 'up she rises'.

Suddenly there's a rush of wings close to my head and a cold wind in my hair. Mr Mac stops in his tracks. He bends his body over the wheelchair and I think he's collapsed again.

'Mr Mac!' I can hear the panic in my own voice.

'It's okay,' he says. 'But what was that?'

'Kookaburra?' I say. The air explodes with its cackling. 'Must be after a lizard.'

'Scared me,' he says.

'Me too.' It's weird, though. A teacher being scared.

A car goes by on the road, a few metres away, outside the main gate. Mr Mac is very quiet. He's just standing there, not moving. Then he says, 'We have both sailed to the edge of the known world. You and I. What lies beyond?'

Instantly I see the dream-cliff. The jelly-road runs right to the edge of a black emptiness. Something pushes me forward. I struggle to keep myself from falling into that terrible darkness, while the road buckles and twists beneath me.

I taste the fear again. The fear of being on the edge of something I don't know. I feel myself fighting to stand still, while the wind pushes and the sea roars at me.

Then the fear comes tumbling out of my mouth like vomit. I can't hold it in anymore.

I talk and talk. About not wanting to grow up. About wanting to stay on the farm. About needing things to be safe and familiar. About the dream-cliff that keeps coming back. Like a warning, but in a foreign language. Like a maths problem that I can't figure out.

Mr Mac's hand is firmly on my shoulder.

'Life is difficult,' he says, 'for all of us. We just get our lives worked out – our ship sailing into calm waters, when up comes a storm, out of nowhere. Next thing we know we're in the sea, swimming for our lives. Not easy. Not what we had planned, but essential for our survival skills. Nothing stays the same for ever, Tas,' he says. 'We have to keep growing, developing, moving on – or we die.'

'Die!'

'Not our bodies – well, not necessarily – but our minds. Anything that doesn't move or change is already dead.'

But neither of us wants to move. We stay there for a long time with all the birds and insects going about their business around us, and the occasional car passing by on the road.

Chapter 14

It's raining hard. Hasn't stopped for hours. There's a tree outside the window flapping its wet leaves against the glass in protest. After breakfast Mr Mac comes in.

'Foul weather, me hearty,' he says.

I nod. 'Miserable.'

'How long are they planning to keep you?'

'For ever.'

'They're sending me home.'

'When?' A rush of hope and excitement goes through me. Somehow the idea of him going home makes my own escape seem possible. Then I realise that I'll be left here on my own. That I'll miss him.

'Today.'

My excitement drains away.

'Fit as a flea,' he tells me. 'At least that's what they say. I hope they're right. There's a certain security about being in prison.' When he realises what he's said he gives a bit of a laugh. 'Wouldn't you say, Tas?'

'I guess so.'

'Well, chin up. And don't let these pirates put anything over on you.' He pats me on the shoulder, the way Gramper used to do. Then he's gone.

'Good luck, Mr Mac,' I call after him.

'Thanks. I'll need it.' The last bit is faint as he turns into the corridor. But I hear it.

After Mr Mac leaves there's a blur of physiotherapy, new dressings, strangers coming and going. On sunny days I go out onto the verandah and play my mouth organ. I can play a lot of tunes now. There's not much else to do. The familiar notes are comfortable and soothing. And I've perfected the trill in 'The Drunken Sailor'. When I get bored, I make up new tunes of my own.

Visitors come, but it's hard to know what to talk about. Nothing happens in here.

I ask about Mr Mac. The girls don't really know, but Mum thinks he's not back at school yet. They've still got The Dragon, then. Pip says she'll ask Enya on the bus tomorrow. I'll probably have died of boredom by then. I've read about two thousand books, some of them twice. And Mum keeps bringing in more tapes for me to listen to. But I have to use the ear plugs so that I don't disturb the other patients. I hate using them. I feel closed in – completely cut off from the rest of the world. As if I have gone over the cliff and I'm drowning in the black water.

Pip and Mum come in together. Dad and Chari are doing the shopping.

'Did you talk to Enya?' I ask Pip.

'I asked about The Dragon. She's still there.'

'What about your other friends from school, Thomas?' Mum asks. 'Some of them have been to see you.'

'Yeah, Reno and Spud came in.'

'Why don't you invite them to stay one weekend. When you're home again.'

Mum goes off to ask the sister her usual twenty questions.

Pip says, 'Mum is still a bit touchy about the Dunleavys.'

So am I. But not about Enya.

The police haven't caught the man who attacked me, yet. They think he's gone interstate. Maybe even left the country. But they have arrested another guy in Queensland. He's a member of that paramilitary group that was stockpiling all the guns and ammunition and explosives and everything. Getting ready for World War III, or something. I try to convince myself that the Dunleavys are not involved. Or at least that Enya's not.

At last!

I'm going home. It's a strange feeling. I've been here so long now that I can't think what home is like. Not clearly. It won't stay still for me to get a good look at it. Just keeps coming and going in snatches. It's a bit scary. Mr Mac was right. You start to wonder about the world outside. Will it be the same as when you left it? Will you ever recognise it again? Will it recognise you?

I've missed Reebok. Will he remember me? Will I be able to get in to the hide-out with my arm in this sling? They say I'll have to wear it for at least two more weeks. Oh well, I'd eaten all my Easter eggs anyway.

Putting on real clothes again feels strange. I have to wear one of Dad's shirts because mine won't fit over the sling. Dad's shirt isn't as ridiculous on me as I thought it would be. Have I grown? Or is it just the bulky sling?

I take my last walk down the corridor saying goodbye to everyone. At times I would have given anything to be going home – especially just after Mr Mac left – but now that I am finally going, it's not so easy.

'Bye, Harry.'

'Bye, Tas.'

'See you, Sarah.'

'See you, Tas. Wish I was going, too.'

'See you later alligator, don't forget the toilet paper.' That's this little kid called Suraj. He laughs like mad when he says it. I can remember when I used to think that was really funny, too.

Then we're in the car and there's this great gulf, widening, between me and them. A part of my life falling away, disappearing over the edge.

We pull up at our house and Reebok rushes out to meet the car. He whines with pleasure and dances about, but he won't come too close to me at first. He's not sure about the hospital smell. I call him again and he comes, warily, sniffing and snuffling, wagging his whole body all around me. Finally I catch hold of his collar and he gives my face a lick.

Pip and Chari come in from school. Pip yells 'Ahh! It's the one-arm bandit.' Then we have an imaginary sword fight all around the kitchen table. Mum is horrified.

'Be careful, Pip!'

'It's okay, Helen,' Dad says. 'He's not made of glass.'

Chapter 15

The longer I stay at home, the harder it is to go back to school. Mum organises for Reno to come and sleep over one weekend. I guess she's hoping he'll be able to change my mind about it. We play chess and mess about on my computer. Reno says Mr Mac is still not back and Enya is very quiet these days. He complains about Dreadlock bossing everyone around and bullying the little kids. I suppose he's still hopping mad about his library folder. One more reason to stay away. Words like 'forgive and forget' are not in Dreadlock's dictionary. And I'm enjoying my freedom. Why can't I stay home and work on the farm. I can read and write. Why do I need more education?

I complain about being tired, about headaches and other non-existent aches and pains.

I manage to stall them until after the holidays. Then everyone gangs up on me. There are all these arguments about not wasting my life. (How come they don't think Dad is wasting *his* life, on the farm?) And regretting it when I'm older. (With my record I'll be lucky to survive till I'm older. Anyway, the world will probably self-destruct before then.)

Correspondence lessons get the thumbs down because Mum would have to supervise them, and she says she doesn't have time. Just doesn't want me under her feet all day, most likely. Granny Anne puts her oar in. Says she wishes she'd had my opportunities when she was young. But the crunch really comes when they tell me I can't leave school till I'm fifteen anyway. It's against the law.

On the first day of term I take as long as possible to get ready. Pip and Chari are a bit sluggish as well, after sleeping in for two weeks. Mum's voice is getting louder, and higher. 'I just can't believe that it takes thirty minutes to decide which one of two identical uniforms to put on! Will you hurry up? It's no use trying to miss the bus, Thomas. I'll drive you to school myself, if I have to.'

As it is she drives us down to the bus stop on the main road because we're cutting it fine. I make a last-ditch complaint about my shoulder being sore, but Mum does not want to know.

The bus pulls up and we clamber on board.

Mr Greenwood says, 'Hello, Tas. Good to see you out and about again.'

I nod my head. I'm too busy concentrating on getting to my seat without falling flat on my face to say anything. Some things I used to do without thinking are a major perform-ance with only one good arm.

Finally I flop down in my seat and Enya says, 'Hi, Tas.'

'Hi, Enya.' I want to say more. I want to say I'm glad she's there, but it sounds stupid.

Nothing has changed. And yet everything is different. The kids on the bus still talk at the tops of their voices. The bus still rattles and sways and the dust pours in through the badly fitting windows until we reach the bitumen road.

The bag hooks at school are in the same place, but someone else's bag is on my hook. I take it off, place it calmly on the floor and hang my own bag in its place. In less than a minute I get a response.

'Who shifted my ... oh, it's you.'

'Yeah, Dreadlock. It's me.' I feel my back straighten. There's a twinge in my chest, but I take a deep breath, ready to front him. 'This is my hook.'

'We reckon you should be locked up for good. After what you did.'

'Who reckons?' I try to keep my voice sounding tough.

Nearby, kids are chatting, playing ball, getting stuff out of their bags. But I feel like a stranger. Like I don't speak the language. Like I don't belong.

Other kids gather around me.

'Show us your scars, Tas.'

'Yeah. Tell us about the shoot-out.'

I realise that Enya has moved away.

'Have they caught that gun man yet?'

I'm trying to get through, but there are bodies everywhere.

'Hey, back off,' I say. I can't think with them all crowding around me. I'm drowning again.

Then Dreadlock says, 'Yeah, give the dude some air, will ya.' I can't believe he said that, but the next moment I know why. As the other kids move away, he moves in, grabs my arm and twists it behind my back. 'This is just for starters.' He jerks my arm. The pain that shoots through me is nothing to the anger that fills my mouth, my throat, my chest.

'I'll kill you, Dreadlock.' I'm shouting and struggling to keep the tears of pain and rage from showing. He runs off with his mates.

The other kids have all scarpered. No one

wants to get involved. Then Mr Mac is there.

'Okay, Tas?'

'Yes, Sir.'

I'm hoping that my face won't give me away.

The siren goes and we line up to go into class. Now there's a huge space around me, as if no one wants to get too close. My desk has been moved. Who did that? I know I've been away for a while, but it's as if I had never been here. As if I never existed.

I'm standing still, like a dummy, not knowing where to go. Mr Mac says, 'Sit down, Tas.' He says it gently. He doesn't understand about my desk. It's his first day back as well. There's an uncomfortable hush in the room. Then Enya comes over and shows me. It turns out she's moved. Her desk is next to Dread-lock's. I can't believe it. There's a new pain. Not in my shoulder. I'm not sure where it is. Sort of everywhere.

Well, if that's the way she wants it. I'm on my own. In the hospital I was on my own a lot. It's not so bad. At least you know where you stand.

At recess time, I take my walkman and find an empty bench on the other side of the oval. I put on the headphones and listen to *Peer Gynt*. At first the old claustrophobia presses in

120

all around and threatens to suffocate me, but then I concentrate on the music. I've just discovered Grieg's music. I'm amazed at the way he can tell a story, without words. The music has its own voice. It surrounds me and somehow gets me in. I see myself wandering through the forest, while the birds play around in the low branches and the sun shines. Then the tempo changes. The scene darkens as I reach the Hall of the Mountain King. His demons are all around me, pressing closer, closer.

Something hits me in the back. I whip the headphones off and turn my head. The first punch lands on my cheek. I'm standing and turning to face them when another punch lands in my stomach. I grab a handful of shirt front and swing my fist. I feel it smack into bone and skin. Someone else grabs me from behind while Dreadlock head-butts me in the chest.

'Dirty, stinking dog,' he mutters. 'Enya should have finished you off.'

'What do you mean?' That's the second time someone has said that. But it can't be true.

'Didn't they tell you? It was Enya who shot you.'

'She did not! She wouldn't. You're a bloody liar, Dreadlock!'

'Suit yourself. But it was in all the papers. Anyway we've got another score to settle just now.'

They've got it wrong. Enya hates guns. But I can't think about it now. My arms are pinned, so I lash out with one foot. My mouth is clamped shut against the pain. My foot connects. Dreadlock yelps. But he comes back at me, wrenches my body sideways and throws me to the ground. My face whacks against the grass with a thump like a paddy melon hitting a fence. Their feet are all around me, their voices grunting, swearing. Several kicks land on my back, my ribs. Dreadlock is sitting on me, smearing the foul-smelling stuff on my face. Then they're gone. I hear them pounding away across the oval.

Chapter 16

Mr Mac has sent for me, so I'm standing outside his office. I've washed my face and brushed myself off. Straightened my shirt and tucked it in. But there's a swelling just under my eye and a bit of skin off my nose.

I knock.

'Come in.'

The door is open so I walk over and stand by the desk.

'What happened, Tas?'

'Nothing, Mr McKinlay.'

'Oh, I see. You get a black eye, a grazed nose and grass stains on your trousers by sitting in the undercover area all through recess, right?'

'No, Mr McKinlay.' I feel a bit stupid. He's a good bloke, Old Mac – the best, I guess. We shared a lot of things in the hospital. But this is school and he's the principal. Besides, I never dob.

'Okay. I just wanted to give you the chance to tell me yourself. But don't forget. There's not much happens in this school without me knowing. And if I catch you fighting, I'll have to suspend you.'

I'm thinking, 'Suspend me, please, suspend me. Then I can stay at home.'

'I must say I'm disappointed. I thought your experiences might have taught you not to look for trouble. Heaven knows, it seems to find you without any help from anyone.'

'Yes, Mr McKinlay.' I stand there for a moment, wanting to say more. To say I'm sorry. Or that I think he's a good bloke. Or something. But he's shuffling the papers on his desk, obviously wanting me out of there. So I go.

The bus crawls along through the late winter rain, windscreen wipers clacking, kids talking. I've made sure I'm sitting next to Enya.

'Is it true?' I say.

'What?'

'That you shot me?'

No answer.

'I'm not mad or anything. I just want to know.'

'Yes,' she says. The word hits me almost as hard as the bullet did.

'Why didn't you tell me? Why didn't anyone tell me?'

Again, no answer. I feel hurt, betrayed.

Then she says, 'It was all in the papers.'

'Oh, great! Fat lot of good that is to me!' Now I am getting mad.

'Look, Tas,' she blazes back. But her voice is wobbly, angry and upset. 'What difference does it make to anything? It was an accident. A terrible, terrible accident. No one knew you were there – until after. I grabbed the gun to stop Mam from killin' him.'

'Who?' But I know who she means even before she says his name. For the first time I fit the events of that day together without any gaps. It's like a puzzle I've been working and working on and can't leave alone until it's finished. Now it's complete.

Enya is crying. Wiping her sleeve across her eyes and giving little sniffs to hold it in. 'I've gone over and over it in me mind, so I have,' she says.

'Me too.'

'Sometimes I think I should ha' let her finish it. Every time Uncle Seamus turns up he's bringin' the Troubles. It was always the same, in Ireland. So we left. But he followed us to Queensland. Then we came here.

'Mam and Da said we should stay out o' sight for a while, not get friendly wi' people – not get known. But I thought there'd be no way he could find us here. Then you uncovered that box by the river and I got scared again. Mam said we must pray, every day, that he wouldn't come. But I prayed somethin' different after that. Like as not Da would kill me if he knew. Uncle Seamus is his brother.'

'Hold on. I thought we were mates. Why didn't you tell me what was going on?'

'But I could not!' Her voice is pleading. 'Oh, Tas. Can y' not understand? Da's no saint himself, sure he's not. Always in trouble at school, he was.'

'I can understand *that*.'

'Seamus stood by him, protected him. They were in the same gang, growin' up in Belfast. Da would never put him in to the police. But Mam goes hysterical now. Says he's fouled up her life so often she'll not stand by and let it happen again. Da doesn't know what to do. But Mam just wants rid o' Seamus – no matter what. She'll murder him, sure she will, if she ever gets another chance. Then they'll lock *her* up and all.' Enya's crying again. 'I am sorry, Tas.'

'Hey, it's okay.' I put my arm around her. There are a few titters from the hot-gossip-mongers, but I don't even care.

Chapter 17

The symphony orchestra is in town. It comes to school to do a performance of *Peter and the Wolf*. We've all paid our money, so we carry our chairs over to the assembly area.

There are about twenty musicians overflowing off the low, wooden stage onto the carpet in front. All their instruments are going squeak, squeak, squark, blah. It reminds me of the first time Granny Anne took me to hear a visiting orchestra. Everyone talking in quiet, but excited voices. The squeaks and scrapes and blarps of the instruments tuning up. Then the sudden, expectant hush. The applause for the conductor, then the music ... wow! Granny Anne told me later that she had expected me to fall asleep. I was very young and it was way past my bedtime. But I was still awake at the end and wanting them to play some more.

Eventually the kids settle down in the assembly area and Mr Mac calls for a bit of shush. He introduces the conductor, who starts by telling us a story. At first I think, 'Just get on with the music, will you?' But pretty soon I forget about that. I imagine that I'm setting off, bold as brass, out the gate and into the dangerous forest with Peter. 'I'm not afraid,' I say to myself.

The conductor is introducing the instruments. The flute will play the role of the bird. It trills the notes of the bird, hopping along a branch, fluttering around her friend the duck. Each instrument performs the music of its character in turn. I can see them all so clearly in my mind. The duck waddling importantly. The cat sleek and smooth. Grandfather limping with his walking stick. Then the sly and evil wolf that makes my skin crawl and my muscles tighten.

The story unfolds with the instruments playing alone, then together, then alone again. Weaving the magic threads of the old folktale around us. Making us happy, sad, scared, proud. When the final note is played, I want to sit there in silence, playing it over again in my mind. But, of course, everyone is clapping, moving their feet and their backsides. Shifting their positions, now that the spell is broken.

The conductor says, 'Now we need some help here. We're all going to have a part in this next performance. We need someone to play the trumpet, the cymbals, the tambour and the big bass drum. First the trumpet. Who thinks they can play it?'

The usual voices shout out.

'Me.'

'Me.'

'I can.'

'Let me.'

The conductor chooses.

'What's your name?'

'Darren.'

Trust Dreadlock to be first.

'Okay, Darren. Come over here and our trumpet player will show you how to shape your lips and how to make the notes.'

Dreadlock blows like mad, but all we can hear is the sound of wind in a tube.

'Not as easy as it looks?' the conductor says. 'How about you? What's your name?'

'Angela.'

'Think you can do it, Angela?'

'Yes.'

There's still a chorus of 'Me', 'I can', 'Let me try'.

Mr Mac tells them to be quiet and wait their turn.

'Now, just pull your mouth into a straight line and fill your cheeks with air,' the trumpet player says. Angela can't make any more sound than Dreadlock, and two other kids have a go. One of them is Bennie. He's the biggest kid in the school. He blows like mad and these little squeaks come out. Everyone falls about laughing.

The chorus of 'Me', 'Me', has died away now. No one wants to look like a fool in front of the whole school and all these visiting musicians. The biggest, noisiest kids have tried and failed.

'Come on,' the conductor pleads. 'There must be someone who can do it.'

The volunteers have all changed their minds.

I put up my hand. I must be crazy. As soon as I've done it, I wish I hadn't. But it's too late.

'Good,' the conductor says. 'Good. Up you come, we'll give it one more try.'

I feel all their eyes boring into me, but no one makes a sound as I walk up to the front.

We go through the 'what's your name?' routine and the instructions again. Then this guy hands me the trumpet. It swings down and bangs me on the knee. It's much heavier than I expect.

There are snickers from the audience and the adults go 'shush'. Lucky it didn't hit the floor. I lift it up again, with both hands this time. It's hard to hold it steady.

'Here, sit down. Rest it on your knees.' The conductor grabs a spare chair and I rest the heavy metal trumpet on my knees. The audience is getting restless. They want to get on with the show. I wish I was a million ks away. Or just safe at home, in bed. I'm wasting everybody's time here.

I pull my lips into a straight line, like the musician says. The trumpet feels cold and alien. I fill my mouth with air. My cheeks puff out as I force the air through slit lips.

'PAAAAARP.'

The loudest, fullest, most satisfying sound blasts its way triumphantly out of the instrument and resonates around the roof of the assembly area.

I nearly fall off my chair. There is a stunned silence, then a few wows of admiration and a lot of chattering.

'Hey, that was great.'

'Do it again, Tas.'

'Bet he can't.'

'Just a fluke.'

'He can't even hold the thing up.'

The trumpet player says, 'Well done. Try it again.'

I'm even more nervous this time. Maybe it was a fluke. I'll look stupid if I can't do it again. But I can't back out now. I straighten my lips and blow.

Again that wonderful, ear-filling sound. I blow it again and again.

They're all applauding now.

'Ladies and gentlemen, we have found our trumpet player.' The conductor has to shout above the noise. 'Now we need someone to play the tambour.'

Other kids clamour for turns again and they choose a cymbal player, a tambour player and a drummer. I'm sitting there on my chair, feeling proud and nervous and ten feet tall.

The conductor explains that he needs three even notes on each instrument and a huge crash on the drum at the end. The words of the song will give us our cues. The orchestra plays the tune and the conductor teaches the rest of the school to sing the song. It's all about soldiers, and a military band, marching through some arches.

By the time I get my cue, I'm concentrating too hard to be nervous. I play my notes like a real bandsman. We sing the song three times to give other kids a turn on the instruments. But no one else wants to play the trumpet.

'Well, looks as if you're it again, Tas. Can you cope with that?'

Can I cope? I'm having the time of my life. It's a really simple, repetitive song. But just sitting up here, on the stage, with the orchestra living and breathing all around me. Feeling the weight of the trumpet, the beat of the music, playing my part. I want it to go on for ever. To be inside the music and to have the music inside me.

But then it's over. The trumpet player reclaims his instrument and I'm surrounded by people. One of the musicians says, 'Well done.'

Then everyone is moving out of the assembly area.

'You were great, Tas.'

'Yeah, how did you do that?'

'Cool sound, man.'

'You do seem to have a talent for it, young man.' This last remark, from the conductor, spreads my grin all over my face.

I'm thinking about it, going home on the bus, and I'm sure I'm two centimetres taller than I was yesterday.

Chapter 18

I'm wanted in the office. Not again. What is it this time? I haven't had a fight with Dreadlock since the symphony orchestra. In fact I can't remember being in trouble with anyone for over a week. Everyone is being ... well ... different. It's weird – but I'm not complaining.

'Come in, Tas.' Mr Mac is sounding a bit tired again. I hope he is all right. 'Sit down.'

I'm still puzzling over what I've done wrong. He says, 'Mr Montrose spoke to me about you the other day.'

I'm thinking, 'Who is Mr Montrose?' But I am getting better at keeping my mouth shut.

'He feels that you may have potential, as a musician. He can't really make a judgement, just on one performance. But he suggested that you might apply for a music scholarship.'

The clouds shift and the sun comes through. Of course. Mr Montrose, that's the name of the conductor of the symphony orchestra.

'What's a music scholarship?' I ask.

'I can't give you all the details, yet. I rang the School of Music and they are sending me the information. But, if you won one, it would mean a chance for you to make music your main area of study. You could learn to play almost any instrument you wish and you would have the opportunity to play with a youth orchestra – if you are good enough.'

I'm stunned. There are words in there like 'opportunity' that I'm always suspicious of, but the chance to play an instrument – in an orchestra. Wow!

But there has to be a catch.

'You would have to work hard between now and when you sit the exam. There is a lot of competition for places and they choose people on their overall marks – not just musical ability.'

I think I can handle that. I don't mind working hard for something I want. Then the crunch comes.

'And you would have to live away from home. In the city.'

The sun goes behind a cloud again and it is very dark.

'You don't have to decide this minute. Think about it. I've spoken to your mother on the phone. But, really, it's up to you. If you're not prepared to put in the work, then forget it. And we won't take it any further.'

Suddenly the dream-cliff is there. The black water pounds on the rocks below. I'm on the jelly-road, trying desperately to stay upright. The wind is roaring, gusting from behind. It pushes me forward. I grab hold of a tree trunk right on the edge of the cliff. As I cling there, in fear of my life, I notice a rope, hanging down to the water. The clouds race away. The sun shines on the sea and for the first time I realise that there is land on the far horizon.

'Think it over carefully, Tas. Give yourself a chance.'

My voice seems to be coming faintly, from a long way off.

'What if I can't do it?'

'I know you can.'

I'm sitting on the edge of the cliff. There are sounds, voices. Through the beating of the waves the new sounds blend together, then separate again. There's a violin, a clarinet, a deep-throated horn. The music swells and fades and I want to be where it is. I don't know how, yet, but I want to cross this sea.

I hear my voice again. My real voice this time.

'I'll give it a go, Sir.'

'Good man.'

When I get home Mum comes in to the kitchen and gives me a long hug. I hold on to her as if I'm drowning.

'Oh, Thomas.' Her voice is a bit shaky. 'I'm so pleased. Mr Mac says he'll coach you for the exam. You'll have to work hard to make up for the time you lost while you were ill. But he thinks you can do it.'

Reebok is curled up on the floor at my feet. I drink my Milo and eat some of Mum's yummy cake. Maybe I *can* do it. With Mr Mac's help. I want to be where the music is. But does it have to be the city? I'd be away from home for a whole term at a time! I was only in the hospital for a few weeks and it seemed like a lifetime. But I was younger then.

I go out and sit in the old tyre swing. I haven't swung in it for a long time. I hold on to the rope and push off with my feet. I have to stick my legs out straight in front of me or they drag on the ground. But the slow, swinging motion is very comforting.

After a while I let the swing stop. I take my

mouth organ out of my pocket and play all my old favourites. The slow, sad folk songs, the rebel songs that Enya taught me. The tunes from *Peter and the Wolf*. Then 'Botany Bay' and 'The Drunken Sailor'. I can never play that song without thinking about Mr Mac and the edge of the known world. It seems to me that I'm always struggling towards that edge. I don't want to go there. I'm scared. I try to go back. But I can't. So I try to stand still, to stop moving. But I keep arriving at the edge, exhausted by the journey, only to find that there is an ocean beyond. I can't see how I can go on. But I can't go back, either. I've already come too far.

We talk about the music scholarship at dinner.

'Wouldn't it be marvellous? Learning to play the trumpet, or the clarinet. Playing in an orchestra.' Mum is beside herself.

'How do *you* feel about it, Tas?' Dad says.

I hesitate to answer. I don't know how I feel. What if I'm not good enough? What if I can't manage, away from home? Everyone will be disappointed. In the end I say, 'I'll try.'

I'm working so hard I haven't got time, or energy, for fighting with Dreadlock. My Maths and English have always been okay, but I never paid much attention in tests and exams and stuff. Seemed to be a waste of time. Mr Mac says exam technique is really important if you're sitting for a scholarship. So I have to practise. I have to do all these old exam papers from years before. I practise essay format, multiple-choice and short-answer questions till they turn into short-choice, multiple-format and essay answers. Or is it multiple essay, short-cut and your choice of three floormats? Anyway, if my marks are good enough in the exam, I have to go for an audition. Mum has read up all the info from the School of Music. They test how good you are at beat and rhythm, how well you can hear differences in tone and pitch, general stuff like that. And they want to hear you play something.

Since I can't audition on my mouth organ, and there's no one in Frankstone who can teach me the trumpet, I'm having piano lessons. I'm practising at Granny Anne's after school every day. It means that Mum has to drive into town and pick me up at five-thirty. But she says she doesn't mind. 'It will be worth it when you're a famous musician,' she says.

'Ring, ring. Mother, I'm just phoning from the Albert Hall,' I say in a posh, Pommy voice. Mum laughs.

The day of the exam arrives and I'm so nervous I put my library book in the lunch order box and my lunch order in 'fiction returns'. A little kid from Miss Watson's class comes across with my lunch order, but it's missed the pick-up. Just what I need. My stomach rumbling and my blood-sugar levels down to my socks.

Enya comes to the rescue. She shares her lunch with me.

The exam paper is a real mixture. Some hard, some easy questions. At the end of it I have no idea how I went. I try not to think about it.

Then the results come back. Mr Mac can't hide the smile in his voice when he calls me into the office once more.

'Congratulations, Tas.' He shakes my hand and puts his other hand on my shoulder. 'Ninety-two per cent overall mark and you've been selected to audition.'

There's an announcement at assembly and everyone gets excited. Especially Enya.

'Did I not say you'd be brilliant?' she crows.

Dreadlock can't quite bring himself to say anything, so he gives me an encouraging punch on the shoulder. I grin and punch him back. I can't get mad with anyone at the moment. Not even him.

The audition is not until November. I'm practising Bach's Polonaise in G minor. That's C. P. E. Bach, not Johann Sebastian. I've been listening to a famous pianist playing it on a CD. I'm trying to play just like he does. Every note clear and concise. Even the fast ones. And lots of light and shade in the music, to show that I can do the whole range of tones. I've always played tunes on Granny Anne's piano. I just have to concentrate on getting this one exactly right.

Chapter 19

What am I doing here? In a city high school. In the middle of all these people and this deafening noise. There are dozens of strangers tuning up their instruments. Coughing, snuffling, shuffling their feet, scraping their chairs, getting up and down. Even the air is tight, tense.

Then a name is called. Somebody Allen. They're doing it alphabetically. I should have said my name was Thomas Alexander. Get it over quickly and get out of here. I don't stand a chance with this lot. All city talk and leather shoes.

There's a sudden hush. Another kid has come out of the auditorium. The question is always the same.

'How did it go?'

The reactions vary.

'Terrible! I was so nervous.'

'Okay – I think.'

One girl bursts into tears. 'It was so awful. I couldn't get my bow tight and my fingers were all sweaty and shaky.'

I know I shouldn't be here. What in the world was I thinking of to agree to this?

'Thomas Kennedy.'

It's the voice of doom. I grip my entry form so tight it curls at the edges, and stagger in through the door.

'Hello, Thomas. And what do you have for us today?'

'The Pol ... the Polonaise in G minor.' My voice changes from a squeak to a deep throaty croak. 'By ...' My mind has gone blank. I know, I know the name so well. But what is it?

'Bach, dear?'

'Yes. Yes, C. P. E. Bach.' I'm so embarrassed. They must think they've got a real doosie here.

'Now don't be nervous, just relax.'

Is she kidding?

I sit down at the piano and the keys are about level with my chin. But it's one of those round stools that wind up and down. I stand up again and a big kid comes and winds the stool up.

'Try that,' he says. 'Okay?'

I nod okay. My voice has totally deserted me.

I play the opening bars too fast. But then the music comes from somewhere inside me and I forget everything else. My fingers walk the well-known pathway of the notes, up and down the keyboard, as if they are walking with their friends. They whisper together, sometimes laughing, sometimes serious. They're enjoying it so much they don't want the walk to end.

But then it's over. The room, though hushed, is there again.

I stand beside the piano and wait.

'Thank you, Thomas. I see from this report that you have shown an aptitude for the trumpet. Can you tell me about that?'

So I tell her about the orchestra and school and some other stuff. She's not a bad old stick, this examiner. We go through all the rhythm and tone and pitch tests, then she says I can go. As I leave she calls the next kid in.

Mum is waiting.

'Well, how did it go?'

I'm still a bit numb. I shrug my shoulders as we walk to the car.

'Was it really terrible, Thomas? It was a lot to ask of you, I know. All those months of hard work. It seemed like a good opportunity. Too

145

good to miss. But I had no idea so many others would be applying. I'm sorry, Thomas. It was too much to ask. And worse than that, it was unfair of me to raise your expectations like that.'

'It's okay, Mum.'

I'm not really listening to Mum, though. I've just noticed all the trees. This school is full of trees. Gums and wattles and pines. The warm breeze waffles through their leaves and the smell of them fills the air. What's more, there's grass. Lots of it. And pathways, but no bitumen. No traffic noise. No crowds shoving and hussling. It's peaceful – almost.

The kids must all be in class. But where do they play games?

'Mum, where do they play basketball and hopscotch and stuff in this school?'

'This high school is part of a huge complex with a university, a college and a primary school all on the same one hundred hectares of land. So there are lots of facilities, but they're all spread out, not all in one small area, like Frankstone.'

'It's not like being in the city, here.'

'It is a beautiful setting.'

'All these birds, and people walking their dogs ... and ...'

'Yes, it's like a big park. People can come

in after school hours and use the swimming pool and the tennis courts.'

'Swimming pool?'

'Yes. The school has its own swimming pool.'

'Wow.' Maybe it wouldn't have been such a bad place to go. And that piano. Would students normally get to play it?

On the way home we talk about musicians, and living away from home. Now it's Mum who is doing a panic.

'Oh, Thomas. I've been preparing myself for Phillipa to be living away from home next year. But, what would I do without my little boy?' she says.

'Mum! I am not a little boy!'

'I know, darling. But you'll always be my little boy.' It's not like Mum to go all soppy on me. But it does give me a sort of warm, comfortable feeling.

We arrive home after dark. Everyone crowds around, wanting to know how it went. Dad gets in first.

'Well, Tas, how was it?'

'Pretty scary,' I say. 'But okay once I got going.'

'When will you know if you got in?'

'Two weeks, they said.'

'Two weeks!' Pip says. 'That's like – for ever.'

Sitting around in the kitchen, chatting about things, Chari asks, 'Did you go to the shops?'

'We didn't have time,' Mum says.

'How could you go to the city and not go to the shops?' Chari is passionate about clothes and can easily spend two hours in a big department store. She thinks the shops in Frankstone are pathetic. But I remember, so vividly, the time when we lost Chari in a huge city store. Mum kept asking people, 'Have you seen a little girl? This high, red hair, very curly.'

Some people didn't even bother to answer. Just hurried away. Others said, 'Try the office.'

'But that's on the fourth floor!' Mum pleaded. 'She could be anywhere by the time I get up there.' That's when I started crying and Mum told me to be quiet. The more anxious Mum got, the more I screamed in panic and clutched on to her. Her hand, her skirt, anything I could get hold of. Mum tried to push me away. Pip tried to hold on to me. I bit her and she yelled. No one could get me near a city store since then. Eventually they gave up trying. I even hate the sound of the little escalator that Dad uses to stack the bales up high in the hay shed. I can still taste the fear, just thinking about it. They've all forgotten it now, and I don't remind them.

'There were a lot of people auditioning,' Mum tells Chari. 'We had quite a long wait. But we did walk through the grounds of the university.'

'Did you? What's it like?' Pip might be doing Commerce at that university next year, if she does well enough in her exams. Mum is putting the kettle on and organising toasted sandwiches for us. The others have already eaten.

'Come on, Tas, tell me about it,' Pip says.

'What?'

'The university, dodo. The one on the same campus as the School of Music.'

I remember the birds singing. 'It's sort of quiet, with lots of grass and trees. Not like the city at all, really.'

'Oh, Tas, it's so exciting!' She sees the doubts written all over my face. 'Well, new and different.'

'He hates new things,' Chari scoffs. 'He wouldn't even change his shirt if Mum didn't make him. He'd wear the same one till it fell off him. It's disgusting.'

'New ones are stiff and uncomfortable,' I protest.

I still can't imagine living anywhere but here. It's okay for Pip, but when I'm away from home I just can't wait to get back.

But I can see myself in an orchestra – one day – playing the trumpet. Pah, pa pa pa pah, pah. And that piano in the music room at the school is something else.

'You'd come home in the holidays,' Mum says to no one in particular.

'Let's all wait and see,' says Dad.

I haven't seen Reebok since we got home. In all the excitement I've only just realised he's not around. I whistle him up and go outside to wait for him. While I'm standing on the verandah, in the dark, I hear this strange thumping noise nearby. I put my hand out and touch Reebok's warm fur. I know straight away that something is wrong. He doesn't get up. Just lies there. His back is stiff and arched. His legs jerk and thump against the boards. His teeth are clenched tight.

'*Dad!*'

I can hear the panic in my scream and Dad comes running.

'What?'

'It's Reebok. He's hurt!'

I'm trying to lift him, but he's too big, too stiff, too heavy. He's snatching short, quick breaths as Dad carries him inside.

'Quick,' Dad says. 'Blankets. And milk from the fridge.'

How can he be so calm?

I race to the fridge. 'Pip! Get a blanket!' I yell. But Mum has already found one.

'I can't find the old grey one, but use this.'

I have a moment of guilt about the grey blanket that's still in the hide-out. But I'm too worried about Reebok to give it space in my brain.

'He's taken a bait,' Dad says, trying to prise open Reebok's clamped teeth. He can't. So he settles for trickling the milk in through a gap at the side of his mouth where his lips are drawn back.

The muscle spasms come every couple of minutes at first. I cradle Reebok's head, stroking him, talking to him, while the milk trickles out of the other side of his mouth and soaks into my trouser leg.

'Stoke up the fire, Chari,' Dad says. 'We'll move him closer.'

For once Chari doesn't complain.

'Come on, boy, try to swallow some milk. Please. Just try.' The tears are running down my face, making his fur wet on the top of his head. I wipe him dry with the corner of the blanket. Mum brings two towels. We slide one under his head where it's resting on my leg. Are the spasms coming less often? Or is it just that I want to think that?

I sniff and wipe my sleeve across my nose.

'Will he be all right, Dad?'

'I don't know.'

I'm struggling to get the next question out. 'Who ... why ... who would lay baits around here?' I can feel anger pushing anxiety aside. 'When I find out who did this I'll ...'

'Someone trying to get rid of foxes?' Dad says.

'But no one in their right mind would lay baits like that, in case their own animals picked them up.'

'True,' Dad says. 'No one in their right mind.' I feel an immediate sensation of hands around my throat, a pillow over my face. 'And if I catch up with them, there'll be trouble!'

I'm still sitting with Reebok's head on my lap. His body is more relaxed, but his breathing is still quick and rasping. Mum wants me to go to bed.

'There's nothing more we can do for him tonight, Thomas. We've made him comfortable by the fire. And got as much milk into him as we can. The vet is out on a call. We'll take him in to Frankstone in the morning.'

'No way! I'm not leaving him!' I can feel the tears starting again.

Mum gives up and goes to bed. She leaves the kettle on the hob in case I want a hot drink or anything. I ease my leg out from under Reebok's head. His body goes tense again.

'It's all right, boy. You're going to be all right.' I stroke him along the whole length of his back. 'I'm just going to the loo. I'll be right back.'

I don't want to leave him, even for that short time. When I come back his breathing sounds worse. I try pouring more milk into his mouth, but most of it runs out. I rub one of his front legs between my hands. A short, sharp spasm jerks all four legs straight out from his body. I give that up and sit on the blanket with my back against the warm bricks next to the stove and Reebok's head in my lap. As I stroke him, he relaxes again and we both doze in the warm kitchen.

I wake up in the early morning. The birds are singing. The stove has gone cold. Reebok is dead.

Chapter 20

I sit for a long time with Reebok in my lap. Stroking his head. Tracing the hard bone down to the soft, dry nose, the wide nostrils resting now.

I lift my head as Mum comes from the bedroom, yawning and wrapping her dressing-gown round her with a soft swish of the sash. She stops in the doorway, then rushes over to us.

Mum is crying, her arms around me, but all my tears have dried up. The numbness of my limbs has invaded my heart and left me heavy, helpless. The others come, one by one, as they realise what has happened. Dad lifts Reebok off my lap, wrapping the blanket around him and laying him on the hearth.

The numbness is replaced by anger.

'I bet it was *him*.'

'Tas . . .' I shrug Dad's hand off my shoulder and stand up.

'It has to be. No one else would do it. He tried to kill me, didn't he? Now he's killed my dog. He said he'd finish me off.'

'This may have nothing to do with Seamus Dunleavy. The police are satisfied that he's no longer in this area. I'm hoping he's left the country.'

'Denton!' Mum can't believe it. 'Do you mean you want him to get off scot-free? After what he did to Thomas? The man is a menace to society!' Mum is furious. 'I know what *I'll* do if he ever comes near here again!'

'I believe that violence can only breed more violence,' Dad says emphatically.

'But we have to protect ourselves. The police haven't been much help. We can't just sit back and let someone attack us,' I say.

'Or take away what we've worked hard for,' Mum adds.

Dad is infuriating. You can't argue with him. He just won't answer. 'We have to find another way,' is all he will say.

'Yes, but . . .'

I still think Dad is wrong. But I remember Enya refusing to be fazed by kids, including me, being mean to her when she first came to school. It worked for her. But it's strange for someone who hates guns so much to end up shooting me with one. Maybe if guns had never been invented, people wouldn't be killing each other all the time. But then, if Mr Mac hadn't been there, Seamus Dunleavy would have killed me with a pillow. Maybe if pillows had never been invented ...

We bury Reebok under the tyre swing. We've tossed around a few ideas and decided that's the place he would like most. Right where the action is. We reject the idea of a wooden cross in favour of simply carving his name in the widest part of the tree trunk.

At school everyone is asking me how the audition went and all I can think about is Reebok. I just want to be on my own, but Enya comes and sits next to me at lunch-time.

She says, 'We had a dog, in Ireland. Beautiful she was. A golden retriever. She had the eyes to melt your heart.'

'Why didn't you bring her with you?' I know my dad would never have left Reebok behind in another country. I'm feeling sorry for Enya, having such a rotten family.

'She was killed on the street outside our house,' Enya says. 'It was when a car-bomb exploded there.'

I feel terrible; sick and ashamed of what I had thought.

'She went everywhere with my Da. He was so upset. He still can't face the thought of another dog. That's when Mam finally persuaded him to leave Ireland. She said sure it would be one of us next.'

When I get home from school, Dad calls me over to the garden shed. The bag of snail pellets has been broken into. A few pellets are scattered on the floor, but the rest have gone.

'Here's our "bait",' Dad says. His voice is full of sadness. 'I've been meaning to fix the door of this old shed for ages. Reebok must have managed to get in and eat the snail pellets.' Dad is blaming himself. But I'm beginning to see how futile that is. Nothing will bring Reebok back. There is no way to undo what has been done.

All I can think about is how much I loved him, how much I miss him. I have come, once again, to the edge of the known world. Nothing stays the same. Nothing is certain. I leave the garden shed and go to Reebok's tree. I place my fingers in the grooves of his name.

I think back to when I was little. To the adventures, the games. And the times when we got into trouble. For getting muddy, for being late home from somewhere. The times when I was mad with him for going off to chase a fox or to hide from a thunderstorm. I stay beside the tree for a long time.

Dad and I drive into town on Saturday. I keep expecting Reebok to be here, tongue hanging out, panting eagerly. Waiting for Dad's 'hup', then jumping into the back of the ute. But everything is quiet.

We're walking into the co-op when a voice calls, 'Mr Kennedy.'

We stop, step back onto the pavement. It's the relieving police sergeant from Midway.

'I've been trying to ring you,' he says. 'We've got some information. Perhaps you would like to come in to the station on your way home and I can give you the details.'

We finish the shopping and go to the police station just down the road.

'Come in,' says the sergeant when he sees us. We go into his office and he shuts the door.

'Seamus Dunleavy was arrested last night by the Northern Territory police, with the help of a terrorist intelligence unit from Queensland. He was wanted in connection with the stockpiling of huge quantities of Nitro-prill.'

'Nitro-prill? That's the refined version of ammonium nitrate, isn't it?' Dad asks.

'Yes,' the sergeant says. 'It can easily be turned into a very powerful explosive. Almost as common as Semtex these days. It was used in the Oklahoma City bombing.'

'I read something about it in the paper,' Dad says. 'But how did they catch up with Seamus Dunleavy in the Territory?'

'They discovered his campsite in the bush and staked it out. He's been on the run since they raided his house in Queensland. Hiding out, living off the land. He knew police procedures inside out, it seems. He trained police dogs at one time. Bit ironical, eh? He has been charged with stealing and receiving high-powered weapons, ammunition and explosives. And there's also the attempted murder charge, of course.'

'Will we have to appear in court?'

'That depends on his plea. We have your statements. Do you have anything to add to them?'

'No. Thank you for letting us know.'

We stand outside for a while, taking it in. Then Dad says, 'We better go, Tas.'

We get into the ute. Dad drives past our gate without saying a word. We turn off to Enya's house. Then he says, 'Best to do these things straight away. I reckon it gets harder, the longer you leave it.'

We drive up to the house and walk up the steps. The same loose step creaks against its nail and I feel the same tightness in my throat as I did the last time I stood on this verandah. So much has happened, yet it seems like yesterday.

Mrs Dunleavy opens the door.

'Oh. What now?' She is abrupt, suspicious.

'Is your husband in, Mrs Dunleavy?' Dad says.

Thank goodness I'm not on my own. I'd probably have run two ks by now.

'Dermot!' She calls out across the yard. Enya's dad comes from the shed.

'Yes?' he says, guardedly.

'Have you got a minute?' Dad says.

Mr Dunleavy hesitates, then says, 'Of course. Come in.'

'We've just heard about your brother, Mr Dunleavy.'

'Dermot,' he says.

'Dermot.' Dad goes on, 'I'm sorry. And I'm sorry you had the trouble – of the police and all. We didn't really give you a fair go, I'm afraid. I'd like to thank you again for what you did for Tas, in spite of everything.'

'It was no more than anyone would do,' he

says. He pulls chairs out from the table and continues, quietly, 'I came here to get away from havin' the police beatin' at the door. Always lookin' over the shoulder, I was. Never trustin' anyone.' There's an awkward silence. The clock ticks loudly. I can hear everyone breathing, each one waiting for the other to speak.

Then Mrs Dunleavy says, 'Will y' be havin' a cup o' tea, since y're here?'

'Well ... thank you ... yes.' Dad is surprised. So am I. Perhaps she's not so bad. If you can get past her riot-shield.

The three of them are talking while Mrs Dunleavy makes the tea. Enya comes in, quietly. She goes up to her mother and says, 'Mam, can we have some of those scones?' Her mother opens a tin and Enya gets the butter from the fridge. She spreads butter on four scones and we go out and sit on the edge of the verandah.

'They're quite nice really,' I say.

'Mam makes g'd scones.'

'Not the scones. Your folks.'

'Oh,' she laughs. 'They're not *that* bad, sure they're not.'

When we go back inside the two men are prattling away like old mates. I have to remind Dad that Mum will be waiting for the tomatoes, to make lunch. By the time we get home, Mum is almost ready to call the police again – to report us missing.

It's Saturday again. Mum and I go in to town because Dad is busy getting everything ready for shearing. We pick up the mail. There's a letter from the School of Music.

'Oh, Thomas,' Mum's hand is shaking as she gives me the envelope. 'I'm so nervous,' she says. 'You do it.'

I tear it open and take out the folded sheet of paper from inside. It crackles ominously as I show it to Mum. She takes it back and reads: '... *delighted to inform you that you have been awarded a Special Music Scholarship* ...'

'A-a-a-a-r!' She screams and throws her arms around me. We dance in a crazy circle on the pavement outside the post office. A couple of people passing by think we're nut cases, so Mum tells them the good news. More people arrive. We tell them, too. Then we head for Granny Anne's. 'Come on. I can't wait to tell her. We'll ring your father from there,' Mum says.

I sit in the car, grinning, but silent. I think about the orchestra, the grand piano, the school with its own swimming pool.

The dream-cliff appears. But the sea is

surprisingly calm. The land beyond stands out clearly. It seems much closer than it's ever done before. The music comes, loud and strong, reaching out over the water. It might just be possible to get across there after all.

My head is full of stuff from the past. Reebok, the shooting, Dreadlock, Mr Mac, the hospital. Stormy times. But things do change, and people, too. *'Nothing stays the same for ever, Tas.'* Thank goodness for that, I think.

'... *delighted to inform you* ...'

Did I really hear that? Mum is so excited it must be true. Then I think about the letter and I start to laugh out loud.

'What?' Mum says. But I can't explain. It's just ... ridiculous ... and funny. Sending a letter – like that – to a blind kid. It's like me printing out this story for them – in Braille.

Jennifer's Diary

by Anne Fine

'Please!' I begged Jennifer. 'It's wasted on someone like you.'

Jennifer has a diary. Iolanthe doesn't. What Iolanthe has are ideas. Zillions of ideas for stories are spilling out of her. But what she wants is … Jennifer's diary.

'Anne Fine is a brand name in children's books' – Paula Danziger

The Drowning Pool

by Will Gatti

Did she slip? Or did she jump? I can picture her now in the pool, her white clothes floating out from her.

Kate and her mother have moved to an idyllic village in the country to make a new life for themselves in a cottage next to an ancient wood. But doing a school project with her classmate Jimmy about the wood's history leads Kate into forbidden territory.

The wood hides strange and violent secrets – secrets with disturbing echoes of the tragedy in Kate's own past, and long-forgotten injustice which only Kate and Jimmy can put right.

Hannah's Ghost

by Anne Merrick

Through the dingy yellow-grey fog she saw a white face and two dark eyes . . . Nothing else.'

'Hannah Mellor! Storyteller!' That is what Patsy Conran calls Hannah when her excuse for arriving late at school gets out of hand. Hannah's teacher doesn't believe her story about Morphy – a strange-looking man who she claimed had chased her – and neither do the others in her class.

Hannah becomes even more lonely than she was before. It seems as though nobody wants to be her friend. Things couldn't be any worse – and then Morphy begins to haunt her . . .

A Daughter Like Me

by Jacqueline Roy

'I'm getting fed up with you, Bess.'
'Not half as much as I am with you!'

Bessie and her dad have been at each other's throats ever since moving to London. The trouble is, Bessie just can't help saying what she thinks – unlike her two sisters, Ella and Jude, who keep their heads down when things start going wrong.

So it is Bessie who gets into trouble when she says the new house they have moved to is horrible. And it is Bessie who gets shouted at by Dad when she says she is missing Mum.

Then Dad disappears. He walks out of the house one day and doesn't come back. The three girls, suddenly alone in a strange city, must draw strength and courage from each other . . .

The Cay

by Theodore Taylor

Adrift on the ocean, then marooned on a tiny deserted island, a young boy and an old man struggle for survival.

This is as intense and compulsive as only a survival story can be; it is also a fascinating study of the relationship between Phillip, white, American, and influenced by his mother's prejudices, and the black man upon whom Phillip's life depends.

READ MORE IN PUFFIN

For children of all ages, Puffin represents quality and variety – the very best in publishing today around the world.

For complete information about books available from Puffin – and Penguin – and how to order them, contact us at the appropriate address below. Please note that for copyright reasons the selection of books varies from country to country.

On the worldwide web: www.puffin.co.uk

In the United Kingdom: Please write to *Dept. EP, Penguin Books Ltd, Bath Road, Harmondsworth, West Drayton, Middlesex UB7 ODA*
Schools Line in the UK: Please write to

In the United States: Please write to *Consumer Sales, Penguin USA, P.O. Box 999, Dept. 17109, Bergenfield, New Jersey 07621-0120*. VISA and MasterCard holders call 1-800-253-6476 to order Penguin titles

In Canada: Please write to *Penguin Books Canada Ltd, 10 Alcorn Avenue, Suite 300, Toronto, Ontario M4V 3B2*

In Australia: Please write to *Penguin Books Australia Ltd, P.O. Box 257, Ringwood, Victoria 3134*

In New Zealand: Please write to *Penguin Books (NZ) Ltd, Private Bag 102902, North Shore Mail Centre, Auckland 10*

In India: Please write to *Penguin Books India Pvt Ltd, 706 Eros Apartments, 56 Nehru Place, New Delhi 110 019*

In the Netherlands: Please write to *Penguin Books Netherlands bv, Postbus 3507, NL-1001 AH Amsterdam*

In Germany: Please write to *Penguin Books Deutschland GmbH, Metzlerstrasse 26, 60594 Frankfurt am Main*

In Spain: Please write to *Penguin Books S. A., Bravo Murillo 19, 1° B, 28015 Madrid*

In Italy: Please write to *Penguin Italia s.r.l., Via Felice Casati 20, I–20124 Milano*

In France: Please write to *Penguin France S. A., 17 rue Lejeune, F–31000 Toulouse*

In Japan: Please write to *Penguin Books Japan, Ishikiribashi Building, 2–5–4, Suido, Bunkyo-ku, Tokyo 112*

In South Africa: Please write to *Longman Penguin Southern Africa (Pty) Ltd, Private Bag X08, Bertsham 2013*